ny b nch of the
 w   ')w

Welcome to the world of
St Piran's Hospital

Next to the rugged shores of Penhally Bay
lies the picturesque Cornish town of St Piran,
where you'll find a bustling hospital famed
for the dedication, talent and passion
of its staff—on and off the wards!

Under the warmth of the Cornish sun,
Italian doctors, heart surgeons, and
playboy princes discover that romance
blossoms in the most unlikely of places…

You'll also meet the devilishly handsome
Dr Josh O'Hara and the beautiful,
fragile Megan Phillips…and discover the
secret that tore these star-crossed lovers apart.

Turn the page to step into St Piran's—
where every drama has a dreamy doctor…
and a happy ending.

Dear Reader

When my editor initially approached me about writing some of the books in the Penhally series, I said that if Nick and Kate were to have their own story, *I wanted it!* Well, you know the saying: be careful what you wish for... And here it is, right at the beginning of a stunning new continuity series based in Penhally's nearest hospital, *St Piran's*.

Kate was easy. Lovely, straightforward woman, with great compassion, devotion to her child, and the guilt that all women feel about keeping the peace at any price. Nick, on the other hand—well, Nick was Nick. Stubborn, obdurate, opinionated, demanding, contrary, dogmatic and passionate. And tortured. Tortured by his guilt, tortured by the past, unable to see a future with the woman he'd loved all his life.

Add into the mix his children—three of them all past heroes or heroines of the series, and the youngest, Jem, as yet unacknowledged—and it all gets a whole lot more complicated! But Kate loves Nick, has always loved him, and she sees the good in him, the decent, hardworking and still deeply attractive man who is struggling to find the way forward with the boy he now has to acknowledge is his own, and the woman who has his heart. And between them they find the way.

It's been a long and tortuous journey for them, and I hope it gives you the reader as much joy to see their resolution as it gave me to write it.

With love

Caroline

ST PIRAN'S:
THE WEDDING
OF THE YEAR

BY
CAROLINE ANDERSON

MILLS
BOON

First published in Great Britain 2010
by Mills & Boon,
an imprint of Harlequin (UK) Limited,
Large Print edition 2011
Eton House, 18-24 Paradise Road, 11707662
Richmond, Surrey TW9 1SR

© Harlequin Books S.A. 2010

Special thanks and acknowledgement are given
to Caroline Anderson for her contribution to the
St Piran's Hospital series

ISBN: 978 0 263 21740 7

Harlequin (UK) policy is to use papers that are
natural, renewable and recyclable products and made
from wood grown in sustainable forests. The logging
and manufacturing process conform to the legal
environmental regulations of the country of origin.

Printed and bound in Great Britain
by CPI Antony Rowe, Chippenham, Wiltshire

Caroline Anderson has the mind of a butterfly. She's been a nurse, a secretary, a teacher, run her own soft-furnishing business, and now she's settled on writing. She says, 'I was looking for that elusive something. I finally realised it was variety, and now I have it in abundance. Every book brings new horizons and new friends, and in between books I have learned to be a juggler. My teacher husband John and I have two beautiful and talented daughters, Sarah and Hannah, umpteen pets, and several acres of Suffolk that nature tries to reclaim every time we turn our backs!' Caroline also writes for Mills & Boon® Cherish™.

Recent titles by the same author:

Mills & Boon® Medical™ Romance
THE VALTIERI MARRIAGE DEAL
A MUMMY FOR CHRISTMAS

Mills & Boon® Romance
MOTHER OF THE BRIDE
THEIR CHRISTMAS FAMILY MIRACLE

ST PIRAN'S HOSPITAL
Where every drama has a dreamy doctor...
and a happy ending.

This June there's a real treat in store—
the first two St Piran's stories in one month!

Find out if Nick Tremayne and Kate Althorp
finally get their happy-ever-after in:
ST PIRAN'S: THE WEDDING OF THE YEAR
by Caroline Anderson

Then read on to see Dr Izzy Bailey be swept off her feet
by sexy Spaniard Diego Ramirez
ST PIRAN'S: RESCUING PREGNANT CINDERELLA
by Carol Marinelli

And there's plenty more romance
brewing in St Piran's!

Look out for the arrival of Italian neurosurgeon
Giovanni Corezzi in July
ST PIRAN'S: ITALIAN SURGEON, FORBIDDEN BRIDE
by Margaret McDonagh

Daredevil doc William MacNeil unexpectedly discovers
that he's a father in August
ST PIRAN'S: DAREDEVIL, DOCTOR...AND DAD!
by Anne Fraser

The new heart surgeon has everyone's pulses racing
in September
ST PIRAN'S: THE BROODING HEART SURGEON
by Alison Roberts

Fireman Tom Nicholson steals Flora Loveday's heart
in October
ST PIRAN'S: THE FIREMAN AND NURSE LOVEDAY
by Kate Hardy

Newborn twins could just bring a November
marriage miracle for Brianna and Connor Taylor
ST PIRAN'S: TINY MIRACLE TWINS
by Maggie Kingsley

And playboy Prince Alessandro Cavalieri
comes to St Piran in December
ST PIRAN'S: PRINCE ON THE CHILDREN'S WARD
by Sarah Morgan

CHAPTER ONE

'OH, DR TREMAYNE, Kate left this for you.'

Nick stopped by the reception desk and took the sealed envelope from Sue, glancing at it in puzzlement. How odd...

'Is she still here?'

'Yes, I think so, but she's about to go. She has to pick Jem up from holiday club. Do you want me to find her?'

'No, it's OK.' He gave the envelope another glance, and with a curt nod to his patients as he passed them, he went into his room, closed the door and slit the flap open with his forefinger as he dropped into his chair behind the desk.

He drew out a single sheet, handwritten in her elegant, decisive script, and as he smoothed it out with the flat of his hand he stared at it in disbelief.

Monday 12 April

Dear Nick,
I've written to the PCT, and will tell Chloe
and all my other colleagues and friends over
the next few days, but I wanted you to know
first that I've decided to leave Penhally and
my post here as midwife. I'm putting my
house on the market and Jem and I will move
away from here over the summer, in time for
him to start secondary school in September.
It's the right time to go, as far as his education is concerned, and I thought we could
move closer to my mother in Bristol.

I'll miss the practice and all the people in
it, but it's time for us to move on. There's
nothing here for me any more.

I would just like to thank you for all the
support and kindness you've shown to me
over the years.
Yours,
Kate

Stunned, Nick scanned the letter again. She
couldn't leave. Where the hell did she think she
was going? And taking Jem away...
He pushed back his chair and crossed to the

window, pressing his hand against the cold glass and staring out numbly at the sudden squall that had sprung up. The rain was streaming down the pane in torrents, bouncing off the roofs of the cars outside, and people were running for cover.

Including Kate. She wrenched open her car door, and as she got in her head lifted and she met his eyes, holding them for a moment through the lashing rain, then with a tiny shake of her head she slammed the door, started the engine and drove away, leaving him staring after her.

He sucked in a harsh, juddering breath and turned on his heel, moving away from the window before he put his fist through it in frustration. The letter was lying there on the desk, taunting him, and he crumpled it up and hurled it at the bin. It missed, and he picked it up, crushing it tighter in his fist.

Why? Why now, of all times, when he'd begun to feel there might be a chance…?

There was a tap on the door and old Doris Trefussis popped her head round and came in with a smile.

'Cup of tea for you, Dr T., before you start,' she said brightly, 'and a couple of Hazel's fairings. I saved them for you.'

'Thank you, Doris,' he said tightly, and held his breath until she'd shut the door. The last thing he could do was eat, it would choke him, but there was no way he could tell Doris that. She'd kill him if he didn't eat Hazel's biscuits, he thought, dropping down into his chair and dragging his hands over his face before flattening out the crumpled page and reading the letter again.

It didn't make any more sense the second time. Or the third.

Maybe the tea would help.

He cradled the mug in his hand and stared blankly out of the window. It was slack water, the boats in the harbour swinging every which way in the squalling wind. He knew the feeling. He'd been swinging at anchor himself ever since Annabel had died five years ago, unsure of what the future held, of which way the tide would turn.

For a time he'd thought Kate was getting married, but then he'd heard on the grapevine that it was over now, and with Rob out of the way, he'd thought that maybe now, with both of them widowed—but then this, out of the blue. He'd never expected this. Never expected that she'd go…

She couldn't leave. She couldn't. She'd lived in Penhally for ever, her entire life. He'd known her since she was twelve, dated her when she was fifteen and he was seventeen, left her at eighteen to go to university, intending to come back for her—but then he'd met Annabel, and everything had changed.

Except Kate. She'd stayed the same—sweet, funny, kind—but those soft brown eyes had held reproach and disappointment ever since. Or maybe he'd imagined it, but all he knew was that every time she looked at him, he felt guilt.

He shut his eyes and sighed. God knows, there was enough to feel guilty about in the past thirty-odd years.

He folded the crumpled letter and put it in his pocket. He could go round there this evening, see if there wasn't a way he could convince her to stay—but there was no point, he thought grimly. She'd made up her mind, and maybe it really was for the best.

He'd miss them both, but especially Kate—Kate he'd depended on for her kindness and common sense when he'd been in turmoil, Kate who'd managed the practice for years before she'd returned to midwifery and become a firm favourite with the mums.

Kate he'd loved, all those years ago.

Had loved, and lost, because of his own stupid fault. His chest felt tight just thinking about it, and he stared out of the window again, trying to imagine the practice without her. His life, without her. She couldn't go. He couldn't let her.

There's nothing here for me any more.

Particularly not an emotionally bankrupt old fool like him. He had no choice but to let her go. No power to do anything else. The least he could do was do it with dignity.

He pushed the tea aside, strode to the door and yanked it open. 'Mr Pengelly, would you come in, please?'

He tried to concentrate, tried to give the man his attention while he described his symptoms, but the letter was burning a hole in his pocket and judging by the feel of it the acid was doing the same thing to his stomach.

'Sump'n's goin' on out there,' Mr Pengelly said, jerking his head at the window.

'Hmm?' Nick dragged his mind back into the room and listened, and then he heard it over the rain and his clamouring thoughts. The sirens wailing, the rapid footsteps as Oliver Fawkner ran to his car outside Nick's window and shot off up the road. He was on call today, acting as First Responder in the event of a serious accident as part of those duties, and he'd obviously been called out to the emergency.

'The sirens,' Mr Pengelly said unnecessarily.

'Yes,' Nick said, blanking it out of his mind as he examined him, weighed him, checked his blood pressure, listened to his chest. He was a heart attack waiting to happen, and if he had one, it wouldn't be Nick's fault. He'd given him sage advice for years, and it was time to lay it on the line.

More sirens. It was a big one, he thought, and eyed his patient firmly. 'Right, Mr Pengelly, I think we need to have another look at your lifestyle. You're overweight, you're unfit, you don't take your drugs regularly, and then you come in and tell me you have chest pain, but you don't seem to be prepared to do anything about it and if you go on like this you'll kill yourself. We need to check your cholesterol level again. It was high last time, and you're still smoking, aren't you?'

'Ah, but I've cut down, Doc.'

'To what?'

He hesitated, then under Nick's uncompromising stare he sighed and came clean. 'Only twenty a day now.'

Only? 'That's twenty too many. Make an appointment on your way out for a fasting cholesterol test first thing one morning, as soon as possible, and then we'll review it, but you need to start exercising and attend the stop smoking clinic—'

'Must be a big'un. There's the chopper coming now,' he said, gesturing at the window again, just as the phone rang, and Nick frowned and reached for it, irritated that the man didn't seem to be paying any attention.

'Excuse me a moment—Tremayne.'

'It's Sue. I'm sorry to disturb you, but Oliver rang. Kate's had an accident, and they're airlifting Jem to hospital. He said you'd better get over to St Piran's.'

He felt the blood drain from his head, and sucked in a breath. 'What's wrong—? How bad is he—is he—?'

'Head and pelvis, he said, but he was quite insistent that you should go, Nick. Kate's going to need you. And he said to tell her not to worry about the dog, he'll sort it.'

The dog? He mumbled something and cradled the phone with a clatter. 'Um—Mr Pengelly, I have to go. I'm sorry. Make the appointment, if you wouldn't mind, and we'll talk again when we get the results.'

'So—do you want those biscuits?'

The man was a lost cause. 'Help yourself,' he growled, and got to his feet and went out to Reception, his legs moving automatically. 'Right, Mr Pengelly needs a fasting cholesterol ASAP with a follow-up appointment,' he told Sue. 'I'm going to St Piran's—can you get Sam to cover my surgery for me?'

And without waiting for her reply, without even pausing to pick up his coat, he strode briskly out of the doors into the lashing rain.

The drive to St Piran nearly killed him.

His stomach was in knots, adrenaline pouring through his veins, and with no one to distract him his thoughts were free to run over all the things that could be wrong, and all the things that could go wrong as a consequence.

The list was hideous, and just thinking it all through made him want to retch.

He called Ben's mobile from his hands-free. His

son-in-law would be there today, in A and E, and he'd give him advance warning. He drummed his fingers on the steering-wheel, waiting impatiently for Ben to answer, and when he did, Ben got there before he did.

'It's OK, Nick, we're on it. I can hear the helicopter now, we're going out to meet it. Just drive carefully and meet us in Resus. I'll get someone to look out for you.'

'OK. Ben—check Kate over, could you? Or get someone to? She was in the car with Jem and I don't know if she's hurt. And tell her I'm coming.'

'Sure. Got to go. See you soon.'

The phone went dead, and he sliced through the traffic and in through the hospital gates, abandoned the car on the kerb and ran in. It would probably be clamped but he'd worry about that later.

He was met at the door and ushered straight through to Resus, and as the door swung open he froze for a second. He was assailed by memories, his emotions suddenly in turmoil. He couldn't do this. Not here, not this room, of all the places.

He had to. On autopilot, he looked around at a scene of organised chaos, Ben snapping out orders and the team anticipating him like a well-oiled machine. A machine that held the boy's life in its hands?

The same machine—and the same man—that had held Annabel's—and lost it?

Dear God.

They were cutting Jem's clothes off, slicing through the sodden fabric, peeling it away so they could get a proper look at him, talking reassuringly to him all the time, and it could have been any of his boys lying there, all skinny limbs and ribcage with only the pelvic binder left to hold his pelvis stable.

Don't let him die. Please, God, don't let him die...

'OK, let's cross-match for ten units and get five units of O-neg to start with, and some packed cells, and let's get some X-rays—a full trauma series, starting with head, spine and pelvis. What about pain relief?' Ben asked. 'What's he had already?'

'Three milligrams of morphine IV, but his blood pressure's dropping. Want to try—?'

The voices washed around Nick, only two things really registering. One was the bruised little face scarcely visible under the mask, most of Jem's head concealed by the padding of the neck brace; the other was Kate, sodden and be-draggled, standing a few feet away watching as they worked on her little son, her eyes wide with fear, her lips moving soundlessly.

Praying?

Probably. There was little else to do. He crossed over to her, and she gripped his hand and gave a tiny sob.

He squeezed back. He wanted to hug her, to say, 'It's OK, it's going to be all right,' but he wasn't sure it was, wasn't sure she'd want him to hold her, wasn't sure she'd believe him—and anyway his tongue was glued to the roof of his mouth.

He freed it with effort and concentrated on the facts. 'Have you done a FAST exam?' he asked, sticking to something safe, and Ben shook his head.

'No, we're just about to.'

'Fast?' Kate murmured.

'Ultrasound, basically,' Ben said. 'It might show what's going on.'

Such as free fluid in the abdomen. Blood, most particularly, from torn arteries, sheered bone ends...

Nick felt the bile welling again, and dragged his free hand over his face.

The radiographer was setting up the X-ray machine as Ben quickly ran the head of the ultrasound wand over Jeremiah's thin, slightly distended abdomen, and Nick watched the screen, wincing at the image. Free fluid. Lots of it. Damn.

They were handed lead aprons. Ben must have realised they wouldn't leave, and as the X-rays appeared on the computer screen a few moments later, Nick sucked in a breath.

Even across the room, he could see the fractures on the left side of Jeremiah's pelvis, the bony ends displaced, the damage they'd caused all too easily imaginable.

'OK, this needs fixation before he goes anywhere,' Ben was saying. 'Are the orthos free?'

'No. They're just finishing off so they're ready for him,' the charge nurse said. 'Want me to get Josh?'

'Please—and fast-bleep the anaesthetist, we need to get on with this.'

'Who's Josh?' Kate asked, her face white.

'New guy,' Ben said. 'He's good—don't worry, I've known him for years. He's done a lot of this—he's a bit of a trauma specialist. But we need to get this pelvis rigid before we move Jem and he needs to go straight up to Theatre if we can't stop the bleeding here. You need to sign a consent form for that. Why don't you do that and then get a cup of tea—?'

'His pressure's dropping.'

Ben frowned and bent over the boy. 'OK, Jem, stay with us, come on, you're doing really well. Let's give him a 250-mil bolus of O-neg and we'll see if he stabilises. Kate, I don't suppose you know his blood group, do you?'

She shook her head, her face terrified. 'No. No idea. I'm O-positive, if that helps.'

'Cross-match results are up,' someone said. 'He's B-negative.'

B-negative? Through the roaring in his head, Nick heard Ben sigh harshly. 'Damn. We used all our stock this morning. I don't know if it's been replaced yet.' Ben's eyes flicked questioningly to Nick's, and he swallowed.

'I'm B-negative,' he confirmed, the last traces of doubt obliterated from his mind with this one small fact. 'So's Jack. We're both regular donors.'

Ben didn't miss a beat. 'OK. Nick, contact Jack

and ask him if he's able to donate today, then we'll get Haematology to sort it. That'll give us two units, and we'll salvage his own in Theatre and recycle it and give it back to him, and we can use O-neg if necessary until we get more, but if we get the ex-fix on, the bleeding may well stop anyway.'

Or it might not. 'You can take two units from me,' Nick said, and he saw Kate turn towards him, heard the hitch in her breath as she waited for what he was going to say. Not that. Not out loud, but he met his son-in-law's eyes squarely, and Ben gave a brief, imperceptible nod of understanding.

A door flapped shut behind him, and Nick turned and looked straight into Jack's eyes.

'Kate, Dad—hi. What's going on?' he asked. 'I was out in cubicles—they said Jem was in here.'

'He is,' Nick said, and Jack looked at the X-rays, winced and glanced down at the child on the trolley.

'Hell,' he said softly. 'Poor little chap. What's the damage?' he asked Ben.

'Pelvis, for sure, and maybe abdominal and head injuries. We were about to contact you,' Ben told him. 'We're short of B-negative. Have you given blood recently?'

'Um—about three months ago? No—just before Christmas, so nearly four.' Jack sighed harshly and glanced at the clock. 'I've got a meeting I should be at and I'm already late. Can you call me if you definitely need me?'

'We definitely need you,' Nick said, his voice deliberately low so that only Jack could hear. 'He's your brother, Jack,' he added, and watched the disbelief like a shockwave on his firstborn son's face.

'Jeremiah? Kate's son? He's—?'

'My son,' Nick said softly, voicing the words in public for the first time, and beside him he felt Kate squeeze his hand. His words hung in the air between them for a moment, and Jack's face was suddenly expressionless.

'Well, we'd better roll our sleeves up, then, hadn't we?' he said after a long pause, and Nick let out his breath on a shuddering little sigh.

'Thanks,' he said, but Jack turned to him, his blue eyes like chips of ice.

'Don't thank me,' he said, his voice deadly quiet. 'I'm not doing it for you.' He turned back to Ben. 'Give me five minutes. I just want to make a couple of calls.'

'That's fine, we're using O-neg for now. You've got a little while. We'll save cross-matched blood until he's stable.'

He nodded curtly and walked out, slapping the door out of the way with his hand, and Nick closed his eyes and swallowed. He'd known it would come out at some time, he'd known it would be hard, but like this, with Jeremiah's life hanging in the balance—

'OK, what have we got?' a new voice asked, and a man strode in, a man they'd never seen before, with a soft, lilting Irish brogue and that dangerous blend of rakish charm and lethal good looks that would leave trouble in his wake.

Nick knew all about that. He'd been like that in his youth; it had gone to his head, and look where it had got him. He almost felt sorry for Josh O'Hara, the new A and E consultant, but maybe this man wouldn't make the same mistakes he had. He'd have to try hard to do worse.

He was bending over Jeremiah now, smiling at him. 'Hello, Jem, I'm Josh. I'm just going to have a quick look at your X-rays, and then we're going to send you to sleep and fix you, OK? That'll take away a lot of the pain for when you wake up.'

Jem made a feeble sound of assent, and beside him Nick heard Kate give a little sob.

Nick tightened his grip on her fingers. 'It's all right,' he said, reassuring himself as much as her. 'He'll be all right,' he repeated, and hoped to God it wasn't a lie.

Josh looked up and met their eyes. 'Are you the parents?'

They nodded, the irony of it striking Nick like a hammer blow. Of all the ways—

'OK. You need to sign a consent form, and then I think someone needs to take you to the relatives' room and give you a cup of tea.'

'I don't want a cup of tea, I want to be here with my son!' Kate said adamantly. 'I'm a midwife, you don't need to mollycoddle me.'

'We don't need to scrape you off the floor, either, and it's a sterile procedure. You can stay till he's out, then you go.'

Nick put an arm round her rigid shoulders, squeezing them gently. 'He's right,' he said, fighting his instinct to argue, to stay. 'You shouldn't be here. Not for that. And someone needs to take a look at you.'

'I'm fine.'

'We don't know that. Nick's right, you need your neck checked, Kate,' Ben said gently, lifting his head to meet her eyes. 'And your feet. I gather they were trapped. Let us sort Jem out, and then while he's in Theatre I'll come and have a look at you, hmm? And in the meantime, go and have something hot to drink, and some biscuits or something. You're in shock.'

She'd signed the form by the time the anaesthetist arrived a minute later, and Kate clung to her son's hand, pressing it to her heart and murmuring softly to him as he drifted off, then Nick ushered her away, leading her out of the room and down the corridor to the relatives' room, his reluctant feet tracing the familiar path.

'You can wait in here—I'll bring you both some tea,' a nurse said with a kind smile. 'How do you take it?'

'Hot and sweet, isn't it?' Kate said shakily, trying to smile back, but Nick couldn't say anything, because the last time he'd been in this room had been in the horrendous minutes after Annabel had died, almost exactly five years ago.

It came flooding back the shock, the horror, the guilt. He should have realised she was ill, should

have done something, but he'd been so tied up in
the practice he'd scarcely noticed she was alive.
And then, suddenly, she wasn't. She'd had a rup-
tured appendix, and Ben hadn't been able to save
her.

And yet again the guilt and the senseless futility
of it threatened to swamp him.

CHAPTER TWO

KATE cradled the tea in her hands and tried to force herself to drink it.

'I hate sugar in tea,' she said, and looked up at Nick, trying to smile, trying to be brave, but his face was shut down, expressionless, devoid of colour and emotion, and she felt the fear escalate.

'Nick? He'll be OK.' He had to be, she thought desperately, his stark expression clawing at her control and threatening to destroy it, but Ben had seemed confident, Josh also, and there was no talk of ifs or buts or maybes, so he would be OK. Wouldn't he?

'Nick?'

He sucked in a breath, almost as if he'd forgotten to breathe for a while, and turned his head to meet her eyes. 'Sorry, I was miles away.'

Miles away? When his son was under anaesthetic, having his pelvis stabilised with an external frame so they could try and stop the bleeding that was draining the life out of him? Where on earth had he been, miles away? And with that look in his eyes...

He scanned the room, his face bleak. 'I haven't been in here for years. It hasn't changed. Still got the same awful curtains.'

And then she realised. Realised what he was seeing, what this must cost him, to be here with her, and her heart went out to him.

'Oh, Nick, I'm sorry,' she murmured, and he tried to smile.

'Don't be, I'm all right. It was five years ago.' And then he frowned. 'More to the point, how are you? Were you hurt? What was Ben saying about your feet? I didn't realise you'd been trapped in the car.'

'It was nothing—just a pedal. I'm fine.' Her smile was no more successful than his, she supposed, because he came over and sat beside her, searching her eyes with his.

'So what happened?' he asked.

She shrugged. 'I was picking him up from outside the high school. It was my fault—I parked on the right, hitched up on the kerb and rang him, and he ran up and got in, and I pulled back out onto the road. I couldn't see a thing—the rain was sheeting down, but there were no lights coming, and I remember thinking only a fool would be out in this without lights, so it must be clear, and I pulled out, and there was an almighty thump and the car slammed sideways into the car I was pulling out around, and the airbags went off and—'

She broke off.

It had been over in an instant.

There had been nothing she could have done at that point, no way she could have changed it, but for the rest of her life, with the stunning clarity of slow motion, she knew she would hear the sliding, grinding crash, the scream of her child, and the thump as the airbag inflated in her face…

'Ah, Kate,' he murmured, and she looked up, into dark, fathomless brown eyes that normally hid his feelings all too well. But not now. Now, they were filled with sympathy and something else she couldn't quite read. 'I'm sorry. It must have been horrendous.'

She nodded, looking away because if she didn't she'd lose her grip on her emotions, and she couldn't afford to do that, couldn't afford to succumb to the sympathy in his eyes.

'I can't believe I didn't see him coming.'

'You said there were no lights.'

'I didn't see any, and I was looking, but—'

'Then it's not your fault.'

She gave a soft snort. 'Tell it to the fairies, Nick. I pulled out in front of a big, heavy off-roader when I couldn't see, and Jem could have been killed. How is that not my fault?'

His mouth firmed into a grim line.

'He must have been speeding, Kate.'

'Very likely. It doesn't absolve me of blame.'

'Don't,' he warned, his voice strained. 'Believe me, don't take on the blame for this. It'll destroy you.'

As his guilt over Annabel's death had nearly destroyed him? She bit her lip, trapped the words, looked at the clock. It had hardly moved, and yet they seemed to have been in there for ever.

'He'll be all right, Kate. He's in good hands.'

'I know.'

She gave him another little smile, and reached up to touch his cheek fleetingly in comfort. The day's growth of stubble was rough against her fingers, ruggedly male and oddly reassuring, and somehow his strength centred her. She had to stop herself from stroking her thumb over his cheek, backwards and forwards in a tender caress, the way she would with Jem. With anyone she loved.

She dropped her hand hastily back into her lap. 'Are you OK?'

His smile was crooked. 'I'm the last person you should be worried about,' he said gruffly, but it wasn't true. She always worried about him—always had, always would, and running away wouldn't change that, she realised. And even though it was tearing him apart, he was here for her now, when she needed him the most, just as he had been on the night her husband James had died. And he needed her now, too, every bit as much as he had then. So, yes, she was worried about him. She could never rely on him, not in the long term, but she worried about him.

'Don't be silly,' she said with a little catch in her voice. 'I'm really grateful to you for coming. I know it's really hard for you, being here. All those memories. It was such a dreadful time for you, and I'm sorry to have to put you through it again.'

'It just caught me by surprise, coming in here again, that's all. All a bit too familiar.' His smile was crooked and didn't quite reach his eyes, and he rested his hand over hers. 'He'll be all right, Kate,' he murmured, his eyes reassuring, his touch steadying her tumbling emotions.

The unexpected tenderness brought a lump to her throat, and gently she eased her hand away before she crumbled. 'I'm sorry about Jack.'

He shrugged slightly. 'I knew he'd hate me for it, but it's not a problem. He's hated me before, I can live with it.'

It was a lie, even if he was trying to make himself believe it, and she felt herself frown. 'He's a good man, Nick. He'll come round. And he'll be good to Jem. They all will.'

He nodded, sighed, and stood up, thrusting his hands into his pockets as he crossed to the window and stood staring out into the rain. 'Oh, they will. They'll close ranks round him and take him into their hearts, all three of them. They're like that. They take after Annabel.' He glanced down at the table, at the mugs sitting there, the tea growing cold.

'You haven't touched your tea,' he said, and she let him change the subject and picked up the mug, giving him room, not crowding him. He hated emotion, and he was awash with it today, trying hard to hang together through all the horror of it. It was all right for her, she thought, her eyes welling. She could cry her eyes out and everyone would sympathise, but Nick—Nick had to stay aloof and distant, hold himself back, because for him, today was judgement day.

And, boy, would they be judging, and talking, and there would be plenty to say. Nick had been well and truly married twelve years ago, at the time of Jem's conception, and the good people of Penhally held no truck with infidelity. When they found out...

Not that it mattered now. The only thing that mattered now was that her son—their son, she corrected herself—survived this, and lived long enough for Nick to build a relationship with him. She wondered what they were doing to him at this precise instant, and decided she'd rather not know. Midwife or not, there were things one didn't need to see.

She pressed her hand against her heart, and realised it hurt. It was tender where the seat belt had tugged tight in the accident, pulling on her lumpectomy scar and the still fragile skin where the radiotherapy had burned it, and she suddenly felt very uncertain. Dr Bower had given her the all-clear from her breast cancer in January, but it was very much an 'it's OK for now' result, and there were no guarantees for the future.

And if anything happened to her, Jem would need Nick. Assuming he survived—

'Nick, drink your tea,' she said, slamming the brakes on that thought, and he sat down beside her again and picked up the mug and took a mouthful, toying with the biscuits, crushing them to dust between his fingers, crumbling them all over the table.

'Josh O'Hara's a friend of Jack's from London,' he said out of the blue. 'I gather he's red hot. Ben used to work with him as well. That's why he sounded him out about the vacancy. And Ben won't let anything happen to Jeremiah—'

The door opened and Ben came in, and she dropped her mug onto the table with a clatter, fear suddenly closing her throat.

'How is he?' she asked, barely able to find the words. 'Is he—?'

'He's stable, his blood pressure's low but holding, so Josh and the anaesthetist have taken him to CT now to rule out any other injuries, then he'll be going straight up to Theatre. And we need to check you over. Come on.'

She tried to stand, and suddenly realised how weak she felt, how uncooperative her legs were, how very long she'd been holding her breath. She wasn't really listening any longer. All she'd heard was 'He's stable', and her mind had gone blank, unable to take in any more than this one, most important, fact.

Relief was crashing through her, scattering the last shreds of her control; she sucked in some air, but it wouldn't come, not smoothly, not sensibly, just in little jerky sobs, faster and faster, until at last the dam burst and she felt Nick's arms close around her, holding her firmly against a broad, solid chest that felt so good, so safe that she wanted to stay there for ever, because if she leant on him, if she stayed there, then surely it would be all right...

Nick stood there for a second—scarcely that, but it felt like an age before he came to life again and his hands gentled, cradling her head against his shoulder, holding her against his heart as he rocked and shushed her.

She must be going through hell, he thought, and then it hit him that this wasn't just her son, but his, too. Emotions slammed through him one after the other, but he crushed them down. There'd be time for them later. For now, he just had to be here for Kate, for as long as she needed him.

* * *

'Why don't you go and let them take the blood?' Ben suggested, once Kate had stopped crying and been mopped up and taken through to X-Ray. 'I'll keep an eye on her.'

'Isn't Lucy expecting you home?'

He smiled again. 'She was—two hours ago. Don't worry, I've told her what's going on.'

'All of it?' he asked, his heart jerking against his ribs, but Ben shook his head.

'No. I thought I'd let you or Jack do that.'

'She'll be disappointed in me.'

'I don't know,' Ben said thoughtfully. 'Maybe a little, at first, but she's said before how well you and Kate get on, and she knows you went out with her before you met Annabel, so I don't think she'll be exactly surprised to know you had an affair. In fact, she said only the other week that you ought to get together, now you were both free.'

His laugh sounded hollow to his ears. 'I hope she's not holding her breath for that. Kate's going. She's handed in her notice—she's leaving Penhally.'

'Wow.' Ben frowned. 'That's a big step.'

He shrugged. 'She told me today—well, she left a letter for me.'

She hadn't even told him to his face. That hurt, but he put it on one side, like all the other feelings that were swamping him.

'I'm sorry,' Ben said, and Nick blinked in surprise and met his eyes.

'Why should you be sorry?'

'You tell me,' Ben said softly, and Nick looked away from eyes that saw too much.

'She's blaming herself. She said she didn't see any lights, and she pulled out.'

Ben accepted the change of subject without a murmur. 'Visibility was awful, apparently, and I gather the other guy not only didn't have his lights on but he was speeding significantly, according to witnesses. He wasn't wearing a seat belt, either, and the car wasn't taxed. He's in overnight for observation, and the police have been in to talk to him already. It definitely wasn't Kate's fault. I need to check her out. You go down to Haematology and I'll see you when you come back.'

He nodded, and walked quickly down to Haematology to give the blood they would process and give to Jeremiah later, after his surgery, after he was stable. God willing. Jack was standing at the reception desk waiting, and turned to him, his eyes raking over Nick's face.

'Are you OK?' he asked, and Nick nodded.

'Yes. Ben's taking a look at Kate.'

'Have you eaten recently?'

Nick nearly laughed. For a moment there, he'd thought his son was enquiring after his emotional well-being, but, no, he was checking that he was OK to donate.

'Lunch,' he said, trying to remember and recalling a sandwich of some sort. He'd left half of it, and it seemed a long time ago. It had been a long time ago. He should have eaten Hazel's fairings instead of leaving them for Mr Pengelly. 'They gave us tea and biscuits in A and E, but I didn't have them.'

'Here.' Jack handed him a small packet of biscuits from his pocket. 'Eat those, and get a drink from that water cooler, otherwise you'll pass out when they take the blood from you.'

And without another word Jack turned back to the desk and spoke to the haematology technician who'd just come to find him. Nick followed them, grabbing a cup of water on the way, and then lay in the next cubicle to his son, the curtain between them firmly closed, while the technician set up the intravenous line and started collecting his blood.

'Can you be quick? I need to get back,' he said, and she smiled.

'It's a good job you're a regular donor, Dr Tremayne,' she said tolerantly. 'Saves all the screening. I take it nothing's changed since the last time?'

'No, nothing.' Nothing except his youngest son nearly dying and Kate deciding to leave the county. 'Take two units,' he insisted.

She tried to argue, but Jack's voice cut across them both.

'Just do it. It might keep him quiet. You can take two from me as well.'

'Are you sure? I don't like to, but our B-neg donors in the hospital have all been called on recently and there isn't any available until tomorrow. Stocks are really low at the moment; we've got O-neg but obviously this is better. You're not still working this evening, Mr Tremayne?'

'No. I've finished for the day and I've got a light day tomorrow. My registrar can cover me if necessary,' Jack answered.

'And you, Dr Tremayne?'

'I'm not leaving the hospital until I know Jem's all right.' Nick replied.

If he was all right. Hell, he had to be all right. There was so much to say to him, so much lost time to make up for. It would be the bitterest irony if now, when he was finally beginning to accept that Jem really was his son and realise what he meant to him, he lost him before he could tell him.

Nick rested his head back, closed his eyes and prayed as he hadn't prayed since the night Annabel had died.

He couldn't lose another member of his family, and neither could Kate. It just wasn't an option. He pumped his hand to speed up the flow, so he could get back to her side as quickly as possible…

'She hasn't got any fractures, but she's sore,' Ben said softly, taking Nick to one side when he returned to A and E. 'Her right ankle's got a nasty bruise, and she's whiplashed her neck slightly, and her chest is a bit tender where the seat belt cut in. The skin's still a bit fragile anyway, after the surgery and radiotherapy last year.'

He realised he didn't even know if it had been the left or right breast, and asked—not that it made any difference, or was anything to do with him, but he just wanted everything straight in his head, trying to make order of the chaos of the day, and this was another brick in the wall he could straighten.

'Left,' Ben said, not even questioning his need to know that stupidly irrelevant fact. 'I wanted to keep her here for a bit, let her rest, but she won't hear of it. She's very shocked, though. I've given her some pain relief, but she wouldn't let me give her a sedative.'

'No. She wouldn't. Stubborn woman.'

Ben smiled tolerantly, and Nick gave a short, ironic laugh.

'Pot and kettle?' he said, and Ben chuckled.

'Go in and see her, she's waiting for you. And give me your car keys, I'll get it moved. It's obstructing the entrance and the ambos are getting cross.'

He handed over the keys, thanked Ben and went to see Kate.

How long could he be?

Ben had insisted she should lie there for a while and wait for Nick, and frankly she didn't have the strength to argue. Anyway, there was nothing she could do for Jem now except will him to be alive, and she could do that lying down in A and E as well as she could hovering outside the scanner room in Radiology.

Once Nick was back, she'd get up and go and sit there, waiting for news, but for now, she was lying wide-eyed, alert, her adrenaline running flat out, her pulse rapid, her throat dry.

'You're a mess, Kate Althorp,' she told herself, and closed her eyes. She wouldn't sleep. No way. But she could shut out the light.

She'd dozed off.

Or so he thought, but as Nick stepped into the cubicle, her eyes flew open.

'Is there any news?' she asked, her face worried, and he shook his head.

'No. I've just spoken to Ben, but they haven't heard anything. Josh is with him in CT. Are you OK to go down there now?'

She gave a humourless little laugh that cut him to the bone, and tried to smile. 'Sure. My right ankle hurts, but I've got some arnica gel in my bag, I'll put it on later. Let's go.'

'Want me to do it now?' he asked, wondering how he'd cope with touching her, smoothing his hand over her skin, feeling her warmth beneath his fingers and knowing she wasn't his to touch, to hold—to love?

Would never be.

'Not now. Later, maybe. I need to be with Jem.'

'I'll get a wheelchair,' he told her. 'Stay there.'

'Don't be ridiculous, Nick,' she said, swinging her legs down and wriggling her feet into her damp shoes with a grimace. 'I'm perfectly capable of walking. I'm fine.'

She wasn't. She wasn't fine at all, but she had guts. He tried to smile, but his own guts were strung tight. He tucked her hand in his arm so she could lean on him, and walked with her to Radiology, glad they were moving fairly slowly. He was feeling a little light-headed and wondering if his stubborn insistence on giving two units had been such a good idea after all. It was a quarter of his circulating blood volume—enough to crash his blood pressure into his boots. He ought to get something to eat and drink, but now wasn't the time.

'He'll be out in a minute, he's nearly done,' the receptionist told them, and they sat and waited,

Kate suddenly even more nervous because of
what the CT might show up.

She thought her stomach was going to turn
inside out it was churning so hard, and the painkillers Ben had given her didn't seem to be helping. Well, they were helping, but not enough. She
rolled her neck slightly to ease it, but it didn't
work. It was because she was tense, coiled like a
spring, poised for bad news.

'I can't sit here, I'm going to have to walk
around,' she told Nick, pushing herself to her feet
just as the doors opened and Jem was wheeled out
by Josh and the anaesthetist. The radiologist came
over to them, nodded to Nick and then turned to
her.

'Mrs Althorp?'

'Yes,' Kate said, trying not to fall down and
feeling Nick's firm hand on her waist holding her
in place. She dragged her eyes from Jem and the
gap in the blankets showing the frame holding his
pelvis rigid, and leaned against Nick, grateful for
the support, both physical and emotional, wondering what was coming, hardly daring to ask.
'How is he?' she managed, her throat tight.

'Stable. No damage apart from the fracture—
he's been lucky, and there's no sign of a bleed from

the head injury, so they're taking him straight up to Theatre now. You'll need to go up with him and sign the consent forms, if you haven't already done it, and I imagine you'll want to wait up there for news?'

She nodded and looked at Jem. She wanted to talk to him—touch him, just touch him so she could reassure herself he was still alive, but he was unconscious, still under anaesthetic. She leant over the trolley anyway, and rested her hand on his cheek briefly, reassured by his warmth but frowning at the bruises as they walked towards the lift.

'Jem? It's Mum,' she said softly. 'You're all right, my darling. You're going to be OK, can you hear me? I'll be waiting for you, OK? I'll be here, all the time. I love you—'

She cracked, and Nick hugged her to his side as they followed the trolley to the lift and went up with him. They watched him go through into Theatre, and then Nick guided her to the chair-lined recess, and the long wait began...

'So that's your father-in-law?'

Ben grunted in confirmation, and Josh watched him. 'Interesting undercurrents between him and the woman. I thought he was the kid's father at first. It took me a minute to work it out. He seems OK—bit distant, but supportive. I take it they're friends?'

Ben sighed and put down his pen, and Josh propped his hips on the back of the other chair and raised an eyebrow.

'She's a colleague as well. He's known her for years.'

Josh nodded. 'I know you didn't always get on with him. Jack mentioned that he could be…'

'Difficult?' Ben supplied, his smile wry, and Josh grinned.

'He probably wasn't quite as polite as that.'

Ben gave a grunt of grudging laughter. 'Yeah. But that's all behind us now.'

'Is it? I passed Jack on the way into Resus, and he was steaming down the corridor with a face like the Grim Reaper. I take it they'd had words?' Josh waited, but Ben obviously wasn't being drawn. He capped his pen and pushed his chair back, changing the subject.

'Nice job, Josh,' he said. 'The ex-fix. Very neat. You're going to be an asset to the department.'

He took the hint. 'Thanks. Let's hope I can convince them all.'

'Giving you a hard time?'

He shrugged. 'Some of them. Not all. I'm the new boy. They're suspicious.'

'Well, they don't need to be. I'll have a word.'

'No, leave it. I'll win them round—I'll bring in doughnuts and smile a lot, work a bit late, you know the routine. A little of the blarney thrown in for good measure...'

'Well, don't expect it to impress me, I know you better than that, and they won't be fooled by it. Stick to what you're good at. Save a few lives— that'll win them round.'

'I'll do that for an encore,' Josh said with a lazy grin, happy that Ben, at least, seemed pleased to have him there. Shrugging away from the desk and putting the Tremayne family out of his mind, he went off to conquer some of the sceptics.

How could the time pass so slowly?

Kate watched the hands crawl round the clock face—a minute, two. She shifted yet again on one of the padded plastic armchairs, resting her head back against the wall with a fractured sigh.

'He'll be all right, Kate,' Nick said, for the hundredth time, and she just nodded slightly and flexed her ankle.

It was enough to make her wince, and she felt him shift beside her.

'Give me the arnica gel.'

She handed it to him and pulled up her trouser leg a little, kicking off her shoe, and he squeezed a blob onto his fingers and crouched in front of her, so she could rest her foot against his lean, hard-muscled thigh. That was all the running and walking he did, mile after mile over the moors, trying to outrun his demons. She could feel the muscles flex beneath her sole as he shifted his position slightly, and the open neck of his shirt gaped so she could see the pulse beating in the hollow of his throat, hard and fast, driven by the adrenaline that must be coursing through his body as it was through hers.

She lifted a hand and laid it against his shoulder, and he went still. 'Thank you, Nick,' she murmured. 'For everything.'

'Don't be ridiculous.'

'I'm not. Nick, we need to talk.'

He squeezed more arnica gel onto his fingers and smoothed it gently over the top of her other foot where a small bruise was starting to show.

'About?'

'Did you get my letter?'

He said nothing for a moment, just kept rubbing her foot, round and round until the skin was all but dry, then he stood up again and washed his hands in the sink in the corner.

She wriggled her feet back into her shoes, wondering how long the leather would take to dry, how she could have got so wet. Standing in the rain, of course, watching while they'd cut Jem out.

'Nick?'

He dried his hands, then like a caged lion he started pacing, from one side of the small waiting room to the other, then back again, ramming his hand through his hair and rumpling it further. It suited him, she thought randomly. The steel grey threading through it made him look distinguished, setting off his strong features—the features Jem had inherited from him. He was going to be a good-looking man, her son—their son.

Nick's son.

Finally he stopped pacing, sucked in a long, slow breath and turned back to her, scanning her face for clues, but there were none. Her warm, golden-brown eyes met his calmly, giving nothing away, as usual. She never gave anything away unless she meant to, and then it was usually disappointment in him. 'May I ask why you're going?' he asked, his voice carefully expressionless.

'Why? I would have thought it was obvious, Nick. I can't just be here for ever waiting for you to sort yourself out. Did you think I would? That I'd stay, to let you see your son a few times a year, in carefully arranged, apparently casual circumstances, so you can keep in touch without having to tell him you're his real father? Or, more to the point, so you didn't have to rock the boat and tell your other kids that we made love while their mother was still alive?'

'Once,' he said flatly. 'Just once. It's not as if we had an affair, Kate.'

'No, you're right. It was nothing so premeditated, was it?' she acknowledged gently, as if he needed reminding about anything that had happened that hellish night. 'We just reached out, to someone we could trust, someone who could trust us. But we were married—well, I suppose technically I was probably widowed at that point, but you weren't. And we did make love.'

And they'd made a child. Until Ben had told him about the blood group, there had still been an element of doubt in his mind, of disbelief. But not now. Not any more.

He looked away from the shrewd, understanding eyes that saw too much. 'Neither of us was thinking that night.'

'And you've done your level best to avoid thinking about it ever since,' she murmured. 'So I'm going to make it easier for you. Easier for all of us. I'm taking Jem away, and we're starting a new life.'

'With Rob?' he made himself ask, even though he'd heard it was off, but maybe it was back on, maybe that was why. 'Is he going, too?'

A flicker of distress crossed her face. 'No,' she said quietly. 'He deserves better than me. I'm like you, Nick. Scarred, broken, emotionally bankrupt. I'm no good to anyone. He's a good man. He was very kind to me, and to Jem.'

He said nothing. After all, she was right. Rob Werrick was a good man, a decent man, who'd stood by her last year during her treatment for breast cancer, who'd supported her through the most dreadful days of fear and uncertainty, a role Nick had sorely wanted to play, but all he had been able to do was sit, isolated from her, and pray for her. And Rob was the man who'd taken Nick's son to his heart and made room there for him, when the man who was his father had found he was unable to do so.

'So was it you or him who called it off?' he asked in spite of himself.

'Me. He asked me to marry him, and I said no. I don't love him—I can't love him, not in the way he deserves to be loved.' Her brown eyes were reproachful, her voice tinged with sadness. 'So I'm going, and we'll start again, and we'll be fine.'

His heart felt as if it was being crushed in a giant fist, but if this was what she wanted, to go, to leave, then maybe she was right. Maybe it was for the best. Easier all round. And away from the shadow of this guilt they both carried, perhaps she'd find happiness with another man.

He ignored the little twist in his chest and nodded. 'You're right. If that's what you want, then go, Kate. I won't stop you—'

'You can't stop me, Nick.'

'True. What about Jem? Will I ever see him?'

She gave a mocking little laugh that gave his heart another little wrench. 'What about him? He'll be fine. He doesn't know you're his father, it hasn't done him any harm not to know, so it won't in the future. I'll tell him when he's eighteen. I can't stay here so you can ignore him at close range. Anyway, you don't see him now—why would this make any difference?'

'Don't be ridiculous—of course I see him,' he denied. 'I see him a lot.'

'Only if you can't avoid it. Seeing him reminds you of your human frailty, and you don't like that.'

He didn't. He hated the constant reminder of what they'd done that night, of how he'd betrayed Annabel, tarnished the memory of James. But that didn't mean he didn't want to watch the child grow up, make sure he was all right—

'How the hell am I going to explain it to my children? They won't understand.'

'You could tell them you're human?' she suggested softly, her eyes so wise, so—so damn knowing.

He gave a quiet snort. 'Oh, they know that.'

'And this is about what they think of you?' she said, her voice heavy with reproach. 'What about what Jem will think of you when he finds out that he doesn't matter as much as your other children—your proper children, all respectably born in wedlock? They're no different, Nick' she reminded him, her words still soft and yet flaying his skin off with their accuracy. 'Conceived in haste, every single one of them. Story of your life. Well, I don't want to be a part of it any more, of the carefully constructed illusion of reality you fool yourself with every day,' she said wearily. 'I'll work my notice, once Jem's better, but then I'm off, Nick, and you won't hear from me again. It's better that way.'

Was it? He wasn't sure. He was suddenly filled with a cold, nameless fear for the future—a future without Kate, and without the boy, this last, unacknowledged and yet still infinitely precious child who, it seemed, he'd managed to love in spite of everything.

He sat beside her, the chairs so close he could feel the warmth radiating from her body, feel the air move with every shallow breath as her chest rose and fell.

'I thought you wanted me to be in his life?'

'I do—but not like this, giving him fragments of yourself from time to time. He deserves more from you.' Her eyes suddenly filled with tears. 'I can't do this any more, Nick. I'm leaving, and that's an end to it. Please. Just let me go.'

Let me go…

He held her eyes, watched the threatening tears

well, watched in despair as one slipped down her cheek and fell to the floor. She never cried. Before today, the last time he'd seen her cry had been the night he'd taken her into his arms and held her. The night Jeremiah had been conceived.

Swallowing the bitter taste of regret, he stood up and turned away.

How could he let her go?

He couldn't—but how could he make her stay?

CHAPTER THREE

HE SAT down again a while later, but not for long, pacing restlessly, ramming his hand through his hair again and again until she thought he'd tear it out.

And then the doors swung open and Lucy and Jack came down the short corridor towards them.

'How is he?' Lucy asked, looking at Kate, avoiding Nick's eyes as if she wasn't sure how to do this.

None of them, in truth, knew how to do this. They'd just have to feel their way through.

'Still in there. They stopped the bleeding, they're just plating his pelvis. He's been lucky, apparently—'

She broke off, wondering how on earth what had happened to her son could in any way be considered lucky, but then she felt Nick move closer, his hand on her shoulder, warm and reassuring despite their earlier words. Unable to resist the pull of that warmth, she dropped her head against his side, listening to the steady thud of his heart, and above it, the tension coming off them in waves, she could hear their quiet, fraught conversation.

'I'm glad you came,' Nick said, and she saw Lucy tense.

'I had to, Ben asked me to give you back your car keys. It's in the staff car park.' She dropped them in his hand, then shook her head. 'I'm not here for you, anyway, I'm here for a little boy who's apparently my brother. I don't know what to say to you. All that fuss when Mum died, but all the time you'd been carrying on behind her back—'

'Lucy, it wasn't like that. It was just once, right after the storm. Kate was distraught, I was distraught. It just—'

'Happened?' she said, her voice a little hard, unlike her usual self, but then she would be, Kate thought. None of them were themselves.

Nick let Kate go and moved away a fraction, and she lifted her head and looked up at Jack and Lucy.

'It wasn't just his fault. It takes two, remember. I was as much to blame. And just as married, really. James had only just died. There was no decent interval, believe me. It was inexcusable, but it never happened again.'

'Not with you, maybe, but were there others?'

Jack's question made Nick suck in a sharp breath.

'No,' he said firmly. 'There were no others. Apart from that one occasion when we were both beside ourselves with grief and I didn't really know what I was doing, I was never unfaithful to your mother. I loved her.'

Jack snorted. 'Strange way of showing it.'

'Jack, leave it,' Lucy said. 'It's irrelevant to this. But what I can't understand,' she went on after a slight pause, 'is why you've never told us he's our brother—why you've kept it a secret for, what, eleven years or more?'

'Two. I didn't know about Jem until two years ago,' Nick said, and their eyes swivelled to Kate.

'So, did you know?' Lucy asked incredulously. 'Before then, did you know? I mean, you are sure about this? That James wasn't his father? Have you had a DNA test?'

'James isn't his father. You've only got to look at him, Lucy. Look at his eyes. Look at his mouth.

He was just like Jack's little Freddie when he was three or four, just like Jack and Edward at his age now. And, anyway, James and I had been having fertility investigations. We were talking about adoption. Why would I need a DNA test? Besides,' she added, 'if I needed any other proof, I have it now. James was A-positive.'

Lucy sat down hard, her eyes accusing and filled with tears. 'So—for eleven and a half years you've been convinced he was Dad's child, and you didn't tell him until two years ago?'

Kate reached out a hand, but Lucy snatched hers away, and she gave a fractured sigh and dropped her hand back in her lap. 'How could I? He was happily married, he had three other children— who was I to throw all that into chaos?'

Jack gave a short, hard laugh. 'The mother of his child?'

She met his accusing eyes. 'Exactly. I wasn't Nick's lover, I wasn't his wife—I was the mother of a child. And I did what I could to protect my child, and you, his other children, and his marriage. There was no point in upsetting all of that. Two wrongs don't make a right. And we've been fine. Jem's had a good life, settled, and I've given him all the love he could ever need.' Her voice cracked. 'And now he could be dying...'

She felt Nick sit down beside her again and slide his arm around her, there for her, giving her his strength and support—at least for now. 'It's OK,' he said softly, turning her head into his shoulder and cradling it gently. 'Don't cry, Kate. He'll be all right. It's going to be OK.'

Was it? She hoped so, but she couldn't for the life of her think how she'd cope if it wasn't.

She felt Lucy sit beside her, felt the gentle touch of her hand. 'Kate, I'm so sorry, I didn't mean to upset you, I'm just— It's a bit of a shock, that's all. And I'm so worried about him.'

'I know,' she whispered, patting Lucy's hand reassuringly. She loved Nick's daughter, she'd delivered her babies—she hated it that Lucy thought less of her now because of this, but it was only what she deserved. She'd given Lucy's father the means to commit adultery, and it was every bit as much her fault as his.

But for now her guilt was directed towards her son, lying there on the operating table, his life hanging in the balance, hoping that when they opened him up they didn't find anything unexpected.

She concentrated her mind on him, focused all her thoughts, willing him to pull through, to make it, to be all right. And then the door opened, and her heart stopped in her chest, eyes locked on the surgeon as he approached.

Nick got slowly to his feet, and Kate held her breath, unable to move until she knew he was all right, but he was, she could see that from the surgeon's smile as he pulled off his mask, and with a leap her heart started to beat again, the slow, dull thud threatening to deafen her.

He acknowledged Jack with a nod, then crossed to her, his hand extended.

'Mrs Althorp—I'm Martin Bradley. I've just finished operating on your son.'

She shook his hand on autopilot. 'How is he?'

'He's OK.' He perched on the chair beside her, taking Nick's place. 'I'm sorry I didn't have time to talk to you before we started, but I was already scrubbing in and I'm sure Ben Carter will have explained what we were going to do. Under the circumstances I didn't want to make him wait. Anyway, he's fine, he's come through the operation well, we've managed to fix the fractures and I think he'll get a very good result. He's broken the two bones at the front of his pelvis on the left, hence all the bleeding, but the pubic symphysis, the cartilage joint between the two halves at the front, wasn't disrupted so he'll be back on his feet quite quickly. We've sorted out the vascular damage, plated the fractures, and in fact it's all come together very neatly. It shouldn't give him any problems once it's healed in a few weeks.'

'So—he'll be all right? He hasn't got any nerve damage?'

'Not that we know of. His left sacroiliac joint might be sore for a while, but it wasn't displaced and I'm confident he should make a complete recovery. We'll know more later, but it's looking good at the moment. We're running whole cross-matched blood into him now, and we salvaged the free blood in his abdomen—that's gone off to the lab to be cleaned up so it can be returned to him if necessary, and then we'll do some tests and balance the blood components over the next twenty-four hours, but that's all pretty routine stuff. Any questions?'

'No. I just want to see him.'

'That's fine. If you think of anything, don't be afraid to ask. I'll be around for the next couple of hours, just in case there are any problems. Jem's in Recovery now, so you can come and talk to him. He's very drowsy, but he's come round and he's fine. I'm sure he'll be pleased to see you.'

Kate nodded, her body suddenly turning to jelly, and she was glad she was sitting down. Nick helped her up, his arm around her as they went through into Recovery, and it tightened as she stood by Jem's side, sucking in her breath at her first sight of him.

He was linked up to a mass of tubes and wires and drips, a monitor blinking on the wall behind him, and his poor bruised little face was so chalk-white against the pillow he almost disappeared on it.

She took his hand in hers, wondering at how small and fragile he looked—somehow so much more vulnerable, with his eyes shut and all the tubes and wires. Where was her lively, vibrant boy, his gangly limbs and eager enthusiasm carrying him through life at a hundred miles an hour? Where had he gone? She stroked his hair back from his bruised forehead with a shaking hand and bent to kiss it.

'Jem? It's Mum. I'm here, my darling, right next to you. You're going to be all right. You sleep now, OK?'

There was a small sound that could have been

acknowledgement, and his fingers flickered in her hand. She squeezed them back, and he seemed to sigh and go off to sleep again, and she felt her legs start to buckle with relief.

But Nick was there, holding her up, giving her moral and physical support. She didn't want to rely on him, but there was something about him, like a rock, an anchor in a world that had gone mad, and she leant against him and let him hold her. Just for now, just while she stared at her son and let herself believe he might live.

'You won't get much out of him,' Martin Bradley murmured. 'He's heavily sedated, and we've given him some pretty hefty pain relief, but he should be more comfortable now his pelvis is stable.'

'So what happens now?' Nick asked, staring down at the injured child who looked so fragile amidst the plethora of tubes and wires and technology, and he shrugged.

'He'll stay here for a while—an hour or two? Just until we're quite happy that he's stable and we don't have to take him back into Theatre. Then he'll be in PICU—Paediatric Intensive Care—for the night. He doesn't really need to be there, but they've got the bed available and they'll be able to monitor him more closely overnight while we balance his bloods, so we might as well take advantage of it. He'll probably move to the ward tomorrow, and then he'll be there for a couple of weeks, I expect, while we get him up on his feet again, and then it's just a case of getting slowly stronger. We'll have to see. The plates and screws will have to come out at some point, as he's still got a lot of growing to do, but we'll worry about that in a few weeks or months. Anyway, I'll be around, so we'll talk again tomorrow if I don't see you later. And try not to worry. He's going to be all right, you just have to give it time.'

Kate wanted to smile, but her muscles didn't seem to work. She realised she was still leaning on Nick, and she straightened up, moving away a fraction, distancing herself. 'Thank you,' she murmured, and held out her hand. 'You've been very kind.'

He shook it firmly. 'My pleasure. I'm glad to see you've got someone with you—the whole Tremayne clan, no less, including Lucy. I haven't seen you for a while. Are you well?'

'Yes, very,' she said with a smile, but Kate could see it didn't reach her eyes. 'Busy. I've got two children now.'

'Yes, so Ben tells me. Well, it's good to see you again, and it's nice that Kate's got so many friends around her supporting her.'

Nobody contradicted him, and he left them alone, nothing to break the silence but the soft beeps and hisses from the instruments, and the distant ringing of a telephone in another room.

Lucy broke the silence first.

'Um—I ought to go. I've left Ben with the children, and Annabel's had a cold, so she's a bit fractious, and Josh is teething, but keep in touch.'

'Yes, make sure you do that,' Jack agreed. 'I should go, too, I haven't seen the kids at all today, and I've only seen Alison under the edge of the duvet, so I'd better go home before they can't remember who I am. I'll come up tomorrow and see Jem, but if there's any change in the meantime, Kate, give us a ring, OK? Or if there's anything we can do?'

'Of course I will,' she promised, and they walked out, shoulder to shoulder, Jack putting his hand against Lucy's back to escort her through the door. And then it swung shut behind them and Nick let go of some of the tension that had held him for the last few hours and looked down at Kate with a fleeting smile.

'I told you he'd be OK.'

She dredged up a smile. 'Of course you did. I just didn't dare believe you.'

'Do you believe me now?'

'I might be starting to,' she admitted, and looked back down at Jem, her face drawn and fraught. 'You don't have to stay, Nick.'

Was she mad? 'Of course I'm staying. You can't believe I'd leave you alone now.'

'Why not? You heard the surgeon, he's out of danger. You don't need to be here, you've got to work tomorrow.'

'No. I'm not leaving you, Kate. I'm here for you, for both of you, for as long as you need me.'

She met his eyes, and they seemed sincere, but she'd thought that thirty-something years ago, and he'd left her. Left her and married Annabel when she'd become pregnant with the twins. 'I can't lean on you, Nick. I won't let myself. Every time I do, every time I think I dare, you let me down.'

'I won't let you down. I promise you, Kate, I won't walk away from this.'

She stared at him, at the serious expression on his face, the conviction in his eyes, in his voice.

Dare she trust him? 'You always walk away,' she said at last.

'I didn't the night James died.'

She gave a soft huff of laughter and shook her head. 'No, you didn't, did you? Maybe it would have been better if you had.' But then she wouldn't have had Jem, and her life would have been empty and pointless. And she needed him now.

'I know I've let you down,' he said softly. 'I know I've let Jem down. But I'm here now, and I'll stay here for as long as you need me, and I'll do whatever I can to help you. Just give me a chance.'

She shrugged and looked away. 'I can't stop you. But I can't lean on you, either. I have to do this on my own.'

'No, you don't,' he said, trying to inject something into his voice that she could believe in. 'And I'll prove that to you.' Even if it took years. A lifetime.

Her shoulders were drooping, and his heart went out to her. Poor Kate. She was exhausted, he thought, exhausted and shocked and traumatised, and it was late. 'You ought to eat,' he coaxed gently. 'Keep your strength up.'

She shook her head. 'I can't eat. Not when he's

like this. Maybe later. I could murder a drink, though. I wonder when they'll move him to PICU?'

'An hour or so? Shall I go and get you something? Tea, coffee?'

'Tea would be lovely. Do you mind? I really don't want to leave him.'

'On one condition—you sit down beside him and rest, and you eat something if I bring it back.'

'You're a bully, do you know that?' she said, but she was smiling, an exhausted, rather watery smile that in a heartbeat could have morphed into tears, and she sat obediently in the chair he put there for her.

'I'm looking after you is what I am,' he said, and headed for the door. 'Any special requests?'

'Tea. And a sandwich, if I must, but no cheese. I'm going to have nightmares as it is.'

'OK. Back in five.'

He went through the door and down the stairs, pausing halfway because he felt suddenly light-headed. Damn. That was giving two units of blood, not drinking anything like enough to re-place the lost fluid or taking in any food—apart from Jack's biscuits, he'd had half a cup of tea,

a cup of water and whatever he'd had in A and
E in the relatives' room, and that was all since
his miserable half-sandwich and instant coffee
at lunchtime. And it was—good grief—a quarter
past midnight.

And the café, when he got there, was shut, with
a sign directing him to the main canteen some
distance away.

There was a vending machine, and he pulled
some coins out of his pocket with fingers that
were starting to shake violently, and put them into
the machine, pressed the button for a bottle of
sports drink to boost his fluids and blood sugar,
and twisted the cap to loosen it. And it sprayed
him.

He swore, twisting it shut again, and suddenly
it was all too much. He dropped his head forwards against the vending machine and resisted
the urge to slam it into the gaudy metal case.
Head-banging wouldn't cure anything.

'Is it broken again?'

The voice was soft and feminine, and he lifted
his head and stared vaguely at the woman.

'Um—no. Sorry. Did you want the machine?'

'No, it's OK.' She tilted her head on one side,
looking at him keenly. 'Are you all right?'

He opened his mouth to say yes, and then stopped. The woman was slender and delicate, but curvy in all the right places. She was probably younger than Lucy, her dark hair twisted up into a clip, and there was compassion and understanding in her emerald-green eyes.

'A friend's little boy's just been admitted,' he said, gagging on the half-truth. 'They had a car accident. His pelvis is fractured. I was getting us something to eat, but...'

She frowned. 'I'm so sorry. Has he been to Theatre?'

'Yes—yes, he's had an op to plate it, and he's OK, he's in Recovery at the moment and then he's going to PICU, but he shares my blood group, and it's B-negative, and stocks were very low, so they took two units from me, and...'

'And you haven't eaten or drunk anything because you've been too stressed, and the café's shut, and now the bottle's got its own back on you.'

He smiled. 'Something like that.' He held out his hand, then looked at it ruefully and smiled again as he withdrew it. 'Sorry—it's a bit sticky. I'm Nick Tremayne.'

She flashed him an answering smile. 'Jack's

father—of course. You look just like him. I'm
Megan Phillips. I'm a paediatrician, so I'll
be looking after your friend's son. What's his
name?'

'Jeremiah Althorp. Jem.'

'I'll keep an eye out for him.'

'Thanks.' He tried to unscrew the drink again,
but his fingers were shaking so much now he
fumbled the lid and it fell to the floor. She picked
it up and handed it back to him.

'Come on, you need to sit down. Let me go and
get you something to eat.'

'No, I couldn't.'

'Well, I'd rather you did, otherwise I'll have to
pick you off the floor on the way to the canteen.
I'm going to buy myself some sandwiches. Why
don't I get you some? I can bring them up to you,
I'm going that way.'

'I couldn't ask you to do that.'

'You didn't ask, I offered.' Her smile was gentle.
'Chicken salad? Ham and cheese? Tuna? There
isn't a fabulous choice, I'm afraid.'

'Anything. One without cheese for Kate, and
I don't care what I have, whatever's going. And
two teas, if you've got enough hands. You're
a star. Here, take some money.' He pulled a

twenty-pound note out of his wallet and handed it to her.

She took the note out of his hands and smiled. 'I'll come up in a minute. Drink some of that before you go back up there, and I'll come and find you.'

He took her advice, downing half the cloyingly sweet drink, and after a moment he began to feel better. Less shaky and light-headed. He made his way slowly back upstairs, and when he pressed the buzzer a young woman let him back in, waving goodbye to Kate as she left the room.

'Oh—were they shut?' Kate asked, eyeing his all but empty hands in surprise.

'Yes. I was going to the main canteen, but I met someone. A paediatrician, of all things. She's gone to get something for us. She said she was heading that way anyway, so I gave her a twenty-pound note. At least I hope she was a paediatrician.'

Kate chuckled softly. 'Nick, you're so cynical.'

He gave a weary smile and offered her the bottle.

'Do you want some of this? I saved you some.'

Kate eyed him thoughtfully. 'No, I loathe it, thanks, you have it. What was her name?'

'Megan Phillips. Who was that, by the way, who let me in?'

'Jess Carmichael. She's a counsellor. She heard I was here and she's been working late so she popped in. I saw her for a while after my lumpectomy. She was lovely. Really kind to me. She gave me a lot of support when I needed it the most.'

He felt a little stab of pain to accompany the familiar guilt. 'I'm glad.'

Kate met his eyes, her own holding that particular brand of gentle reproach that she reserved for him. 'I could have done with your support then, too, Nick.'

He looked away, swamped with regret, but what could he have done? 'You had Rob,' he reminded her.

'That didn't exclude you.'

Oh, it did. 'I didn't want to get in the way,' he said. 'He seemed genuinely decent, very fond of you—I thought you might stand a chance of happiness, a future for you and Jeremiah with a man you loved. A man who could love you back. I didn't want to get in the way of that.'

'You wouldn't have done,' she reasoned, remembering how it had felt when he'd kept his distance—Nick, the only man she'd ever really loved, keeping her at arm's length when all she'd really wanted was for him to hold her and tell her it would be all right. Tell her that if it wouldn't, he'd be there for their son. 'You wouldn't have been in the way,' she told him, realising, even as she said it, that of course he would have been.

'You know that's not true,' he said gently, and she shook her head.

'Nick, I needed you—even if you weren't with me, I needed to know that you cared, but you never said a thing.' She laughed, but it came out slightly bitterly with the remembered hurt. 'I thought you'd brought me flowers, but they were from everyone at the practice, you were just the messenger.'

He gave her a wintry smile. 'Would you have accepted them if they'd been from me?'

And then she knew—realised, with sudden insight, that they had been from him—been his idea, his choice, probably even paid for himself. And him bringing them had been the nearest he could get to telling her that he was thinking of her, worrying about her.

That he cared.

He hadn't let her down, he'd just given her

space, stepped back out of Rob's way. And she'd misunderstood.

Her eyes filled, and she nodded, just once. 'Yes,' she said. 'Yes, I would have accepted them. Thank you.'

'Don't thank me,' he said gruffly. 'I did nothing—just as I always do nothing. If I'd acknowledged Jeremiah sooner, if I'd done what I should have done, then I would have been supporting you financially, making sure you had a safer car, a car with side impact protection instead of a little tin box that crushed like an eggshell—'

'No!' she said, reaching for his hand, clutching hold of it so he couldn't avoid her, her voice no more than an urgent whisper in the quiet room. 'I won't let you do that! This is not your fault. This is my fault, my guilt, and I'm damned if I'll let you have it and add it to the endless layers that you hide behind! I had the crash, I bought the car—'

'Because of me,' he returned stubbornly. 'Because I didn't accept that he was my son. Because I was letting you down again, hiding from the truth, hoping it would go away, but it won't, will it? But you are, and you're taking my son with you.'

And he didn't want her to, he realised. He really, really didn't want her to.

He turned his back on her, and saw Megan Phillips at the door, beckoning to him. 'Looks like our food's here,' he said curtly, and went out.

Kate followed him, and the woman smiled at her.

'You must be Nick's friend. I'm Megan Phillips, one of the paediatric registrars,' she said. 'I'll be looking after Jem when he's in PICU and on the ward later. How's he doing?'

'He's all right. He's going to be all right. Mr Bradley said it's just routine now,' she said, trying to inject some conviction into her voice, and as she did so she realised that for the first time she believed that he might be all right, that he might turn the corner, might actually make it, and the relief nearly took her legs out from under her.

Megan handed over the food she'd brought up for them, gave Nick his change and then left them to it. Nick opened Kate's sandwich and handed it to her, pushing her into a chair.

'Eat that before you collapse,' he ordered gruffly, ripping open another packet and demolishing the contents, then he drained his tea and dropped his head back, rolling it towards her with a sigh. 'You're not eating, Kate. Come on. You need to keep your strength up.'

'I can't eat.'

'Come on, you promised.'

She nodded. She had, and he wouldn't give up until she'd eaten the darned sandwich, she knew that, so she took a bite, and he stopped watching her like a hawk and glanced at his watch.

'I need to make a call.'

'A call?' she asked, realising she hadn't told her mother yet. Or Chloe, or Rob. She ought to tell them Jem was all right—but not now. Not in the middle of the night. She'd call them tomorrow—except…

'Oh, Nick, the dog. I need to make arrangements. I hadn't even thought about it.'

'It's OK. Oliver said not to worry, they'll sort it.'

'Bless them. They're so kind.' She sighed with relief, then looked at her watch. 'Nick, it's awfully late. Who are you ringing?'

'Edward.'

His other son, currently in South America and still, presumably, unaware. 'Oh. Oh, Nick.'

She reached for his hand and he squeezed hers reassuringly.

'Hey, I'm fine. I'll be back in a minute. Eat, and have some tea. It's just the right temperature.'

She nodded, and forced herself to finish the sandwich and drink some of the tea before going back into Recovery to sit by Jem's bedside.

They'd been monitoring him constantly, checking him every few minutes, and as she went back in, they told her he was ready to go through to PICU.

'We'll find you a bed if you like—are you staying?' the nurse who was moving him asked her, and she nodded.

'Yes—if I can. I'll sit in the chair beside him, though. I don't need a bed.'

'We'll see. Let's take him and get him settled, and you can decide then, but he's stable now and he'll sleep all night; if you take my advice, you'll get your head down, because he'll need you when he wakes up and being the parent of a sick child is very wearing. You'll need your rest if you're going to be any good to him.'

Sensible advice, but she wasn't happy to take it. She wanted to be beside Jem, couldn't bear to leave his side, and even if she did, she didn't think she'd sleep.

'Kate, you were in the accident, too, you need to rest,' Nick said firmly when she continued to protest to the PICU nurse after he was settled. 'I'll sit with him. Go and have an hour, at least.'

'Half an hour,' she conceded, giving in because she knew it made sense and she was at the end of her tether. And the nurse was right—if she was going to be any use to Jem, she needed some sleep. 'I could do with lying down. What about you? Are you feeling better? Less shaky since you ate?'

'I'm fine,' he said, telling her nothing, as usual.

'Did you get hold of Edward?'

He shook his head. 'Go on, go and lie down. I'll get you if there's the slightest change.'

'Promise.'

'I promise,' he said, and she didn't know why, but she believed him. Maybe because she had no choice. Or maybe because this time, at least, she knew she could trust him?

So she went, escorted to a tiny room nearby just big enough for a chair, a little bedside locker and a bed made up with crisp white hospital linen.

She'd never been more pleased to see a bed in her life. Her neck was a little sore, she had a killer headache, probably from the stress, her ankle was aching where the pedal had been squashed into it and she was emotionally exhausted.

She took some of the painkillers Ben had given her, then crept under the covers with a shaky sigh. Oh, that was better. Half an hour of this and she'd be able to cope again. Rolling to her side, she closed her eyes and lay there in the quiet room, and as the tension drained out of her, the only thing that had held her together up to now, she gave a tiny sob and tears leaked silently out of the corners of her eyes and dribbled down onto the pillow as she lay there.

Jem was all right. He'd be all right. He would.

She told herself the same thing, over and over again like a mantra, and gradually she fell into a shallow, restless sleep.

CHAPTER FOUR

NICK closed the door softly and stood looking down at her.

He didn't want to wake her, but he'd promised her he would, and she'd had over three hours, not just the half hour she'd agreed to.

But she was sleeping so deeply, curled on her side with one hand tucked under her cheek, and she looked defenceless and vulnerable. He perched on the hard plastic chair by the bed and watched her sleep for a moment, then with a quiet sigh he leant forwards and stroked her hair. She didn't stir, and he let his hand fall to the pillow.

And frowned. It was wet, and in the soft glow from the bedside light he could see a damp stain under the edge of her cheek, below her eye. Salt trails had dried across her temple, and down over her nose from the other eye, and he realised she'd been crying in her sleep. He closed his eyes and took a slow, steadying breath, then touched her again.

'Kate?'

Her eyes flew open, and she started to sit up. 'What is it? What's wrong?'

'Nothing,' he said hastily, kicking himself for scaring her. 'It's all right, he's fine. He's asleep, but you asked me to wake you.'

She let her breath out on a shaky little sigh, and dropped back against the pillows. 'Oh. Sorry. I must have dozed off— What time is it?'

'Twenty to five.'

'Five!'

She sat up again, pushed back the covers and slid to her feet, swaying slightly. 'Steady,' he murmured, standing up and putting his arms around her to support her, and she rested her head against his shoulder with a sigh.

'How's your neck?' he asked, and she gave a little shrug.

'OK.'

He was pretty sure it wasn't. A bang hard enough to do that to Jem must have shaken her up, and he slid his hand carefully around the back of her neck and massaged the taut, tired muscles under the soft waterfall of dark hair. She shifted so her forehead was propped against his chest, just above his heart, and if he'd bent his head a fraction he could have dropped a kiss on her hair.

But he wouldn't. Of course he wouldn't. She wouldn't want it, and he wouldn't embarrass her by doing anything so stupid, but he held her head, his hand curved protectively round it, steadying her as his fingers worked slowly, gently on the muscles.

'Better?' he asked, and she nodded slightly, so he eased back and let her straighten before he moved away. 'Go and sit with him and I'll get us a coffee. Do you want anything else?'

'Tea. Tea would be lovely, and maybe a pastry or something. Thanks, Nick.'

'Any time,' he said, and backed away, leaving her to straighten her clothes and freshen up while he made the round trip to the canteen. He could do with stretching his legs, and a change of scene wouldn't hurt after hours of staring at his son's bruised and swollen face and wondering how the hell to tell him he was his father.

More to the point, wondering what Jeremiah would make of the news. He suspected not a lot. All in all, it was probably shaping up to be another thoroughly bloody day...

* * *

She sent Nick to lie down when he got back with the hot drinks and pastries, and he nodded and went without a word. He looked exhausted, she thought. Drained and stressed and emotionally threadbare.

She'd never seen him like this, even when he'd lost Annabel. He desperately needed a shave, and for a man who usually dressed so fastidiously, he was falling apart. His shirt was creased and open at the neck, the tie long gone, and his usually immaculate suit was crumpled and weary.

And despite it all, he was still the best-looking man she'd ever seen, the only man she'd ever really wanted. Apart from necessity he hadn't left her side since he'd arrived in Resus, and she didn't know how she would have got through it without him.

Although, of course, even though the biggest hurdle had been overcome in that Jeremiah was still alive, there was still the next obstacle to deal with, the one they'd been avoiding now for years, and she had no idea how Nick would be when the time came. One thing she knew for sure, he couldn't bottle out now, and maybe it wasn't the right time to go away. Her letter to the PCT was still in her bag, waiting for her to post it after she'd picked Jem up, only of course that had never happened, and now...

Oh, what on earth should she do? It had been complicated enough before this, but now...

She sipped her tea, hands cradling the paper cup, fingers tracing the ribbed cardboard holder round it, chafing it rhythmically as she sat with glazed eyes fixed on her sleeping son, watching the slow rise and fall of his chest, the occasional flutter of his eyelids, the trace of his heartbeat on the monitor, and prayed that when the time came, he could forgive them both for what they'd done to him.

They woke Jem at six, when they came to check his obs, and he smiled at her a little wanly. She'd never been so pleased to see his smile in her life.

'Mum,' he croaked, and she felt her eyes well with tears.

'Hello, darling. Good morning.' She leant forwards and took his free hand, the one that wasn't wired up to the drip, and kissed his bruised cheek gently. She'd studied his notes, and he'd had several units of blood overnight. She wondered if any of them had been Nick's, if his father's blood was now circulating in his veins. Or Jack's.

Like blood brothers cutting themselves and swapping blood, but on a grander scale and one-way. Would it bring them all closer? She hoped so. Apart from her mother in Bristol, and James's brother, the man Jem called Uncle John, there was no other family. It would be nice for him to have the family he should have had all along, but she wasn't going to make assumptions. Maybe they wouldn't want that level of involvement. She couldn't blame them. And there was still that hurdle to overcome, of course.

She stroked her thumb lightly over the back of his hand, and his fingers tightened a little. 'What time is it?'

'Six in the morning.'

'Oh.' He thought about that for a moment, then gave a tiny sigh. 'Can I have a drink? My throat's sore and my mouth's really dry.'

She glanced up. He was still nil by mouth, but she could give him a mouthwash. She spoke to the nurse, and a minute later she was swabbing his lips with the cool liquid, wiping away the dried secretions so he'd be more comfortable. 'Better?' she asked, and he smiled and nodded.

'Mmm. I'm sore all over, Mum.'

Her heart contracted. 'I bet you are, my love.

You've been through the wringer. Do you remember what happened yesterday?' she asked him softly.

He shook his head. 'No. The last thing I remember was making you a pot.' He frowned. 'Did I tell you I'd made you a pot?'

She nodded, thinking it might have been the last thing he'd done, the last thing he'd said to her, and she struggled not to cry. 'Yes, you did. A yellow one. I'm looking forward to seeing it. Do you remember me picking you up? Or the helicopter?'

He shook his head. 'Helicopter? No. I don't remember anything after making the pot. Did I go in a helicopter?'

'Yes. The air ambulance brought you here.'

'And I don't remember,' he mumbled, looking disgusted. 'I've always wanted to go in a helicopter. So what happened to me? Why am I so sore? Did we have a car accident?'

'Yes. I pulled out, and—'

She broke off, just as Nick appeared on the other side of the bed. 'Someone was going too fast,' he said firmly, 'and ran into the side of the car. It was his fault.'

'Oh,' he said, but she could see he was flagging.

'I can't believe I don't remember the helicopter,' he mumbled drowsily, and then looked at Nick and his brows clumped together in a little frown. 'Uncle Nick, why haven't you shaved today?'

She heard the quiet rasp as he scrubbed his hand over his jaw. Emotions chased across his face, and he pressed his lips together briefly. 'I haven't had a chance, I've been here all night,' he said. 'We both have.'

'Really? Why?'

Because you were sick. Because we thought you were going to die—

Kate met his eyes, and Nick reached out and brushed his knuckles over his son's thin, pale cheek and tried to smile. 'We were worried about you. You've been pretty sick. You had to have an operation.'

'Why did I need an operation? I don't really understand. I'm just really sore all over and I can't move, it hurts too much.'

Her fingers tightened involuntarily. 'I know. The surgeon will come and see you later—he'll explain. You had some broken bones, and they had to fix the ends together, to keep them still so they can heal and stop them hurting.'

He frowned. 'I can remember it hurting,' he said

slowly. 'Much worse than this. And Ben—was Ben there?'

'Ben was there,' Nick confirmed. 'Don't worry about it, it's all over now and you're on the mend. You just need to rest and get well again, and then you'll be able to go home.'

'When?'

Kate swallowed. 'Not for a little while.'

His face fell. 'I'm going to miss the rest of holiday club, aren't I?' he said, looking worried, and she nodded.

'I'm afraid so. You could be in here for a few weeks.'

'Oh. Can Matt get my pot for you? Will you ask him?'

'You can ask him yourself. I'm sure he'll come and visit you soon.'

She saw Nick stiffen, but she couldn't pander to his feelings. Rob and his son Matt were an important part of Jem's life, and although she wasn't going to marry Rob, she wasn't going to avoid him, either, or his son. For Jem's sake, he needed to keep some continuity in his life.

Nick would just have to get over it.

Martin Bradley came to see Jem just before eight, and decided he could be moved into a side room on the paediatric ward just down the corridor as soon as it was cleared.

'You're doing really well, we're very pleased, so you can have a nice room to yourself for a few days so you can rest quietly until you're feeling a bit brighter, then we'll move you down into the other ward with kids of your own age, to give you some company. I'm going to increase your pain relief, because you're obviously quite sore, and once you're a bit more comfortable you'll feel a lot better.'

'Thanks,' Jem murmured, and his eyes flicked past Kate to the door, and he grinned weakly. 'Hey, Ben,' he said, and Ben came into the room and perched on the end of the bed.

'Hi, tiger. So, how is he, Martin? Will he live?'

'Oh, I reckon. Nice work, that pelvic fixator, made my job a lot easier. Did you do it?'

'No, that was Josh O'Hara. He's going to be a real asset. I had a look at the X-rays—it's looking good.'

'Mmm. It went back nicely. I'm pleased. Well, I'll leave you all to it. I'll catch up with you later, Jem.'

'So, how's it feeling, young'un?' Ben asked, and the boy shrugged.

'Sore.'

'Yeah, I'll bet. Still, you'll soon be up and about. Look on the bright side, you won't have to go to school for a few weeks.'

Kate frowned. Of course he wouldn't. And that meant she wouldn't be able to go to work, because there was no way she was leaving him with anyone else until he was better.

'Kate, don't worry, they'll get cover,' Nick said softly, reading her mind. 'I'm going to have to go in and sort it all out shortly, but you're not to worry, it'll be fine.'

She nodded. Of course it would be, but there were so many patients she wanted to be there for—Gemma was a few days overdue now and she didn't want to hand her over at this stage; she was one of their own, a practice nurse who was married to one of their GPs, Sam Cavendish, and Kate hated the fact that she'd have to bail on them at this stage. And there was a woman she'd seen—heavens, only yesterday—who she'd been a bit worried about. She couldn't even remember her name, but Chloe would sort it for her. As the only other midwife based in the practice, she'd have to.

'Nick, I need to speak to Chloe. There's a patient—'

'I'll get her to come and see you. She'll want to, anyway. They all will.'

Of course they would. They were a fabulous bunch of people, and she didn't know how she would have got through the last year without their support. She nodded, and turned back to Ben, who was making Jem laugh weakly with a dreadful joke. She smiled at him, and he winked and stood up.

'I need to get back to work, but I just thought I'd come and touch base. And Lucy'll be in later. She's going to leave the kids with me at lunchtime and slip up for a minute. You might want to shave by then.'

His teasing eyes met Nick's, and Kate thought she could read reassurance and support in them. Had Lucy come round? Maybe Ben had been able to listen to her and let her talk it all through last night, and maybe she'd softened her stance a little. Goodness, she hoped so. She didn't care if Lucy never forgave her for her part in it, but that she shouldn't forgive Nick—that was unthinkable.

She was his little girl, the apple of his eye, and he adored her. He'd be gutted if there was a permanent rift between them.

And then, when Ben had hardly left the room, Jack came in and grinned at Jem and perched on the end of the bed where Ben had sat.

'Hi there, kiddo. How're you doing?'

'OK. Bit sore.'

'I'll bet.' Jack glanced up at his father, and winced at the state of him. 'Dad, you look like a tramp. I think you need a shower and a shave. I've got a clean shirt here—do you want it?'

'No, it's OK, I'm going to go shortly and sort some stuff out at the surgery, so I'll have a shower then. Thanks, anyway.'

'Don't thank me, I just didn't want you scaring the children,' he said, but this time his voice was kinder, less condemnatory than the last time he'd told his father not to thank him, over the blood donating issue, and Nick gave a wry smile.

After a few moments of banter, Jack, too, left them alone, and it wasn't long before the nurses came to move Jem through to the paediatric ward.

'All ready to go?' the staff nurse asked cheerfully, and he nodded as they kicked the brakes off the bed and wheeled it through the door, down a corridor and then into a bright, sunny room off the children's ward that looked out over the gardens below.

'There are ducks down there,' Kate told him, peering out of the window and trying to find something normal to talk about as they sorted out his oxygen and monitoring equipment and pushed his locker back into place. 'A mother duck and some ducklings. You'll be able to see them when you can move around a bit more.'

'How many ducklings?' he asked, but she couldn't really tell.

'At least five. Not sure. We'll count them together later. They can't go anywhere, they're in a courtyard.'

'What, trapped?'

'Until they can fly. I expect someone's looking after them, but they'll be safe from any cats and foxes, at least.'

'Mmm.'

His eyelids were wilting, and it was obvious he was still very far from well. The move from PICU to the little side room had been more than enough for him, and Nick glanced at his watch. Ten-fifteen, give or take.

'I need to go to the surgery, sort a few things out, and if you're staying, you could do with some clothes and wash things, and some stuff for Jeremiah. Give me your keys, I'll sort it.'

She stared at him blankly. 'I haven't got my keys,' she said slowly. 'They must be in the car still.'

'Has anyone else got a key?'

She nodded. 'Yes. Chloe. Take her with you, she'll know what to get. And tell her I'm sorry about Bruno. If she can't manage, then I'll have to—'

'I'm sure they can manage the dog between them,' he said reassuringly. 'They said you weren't to worry. I'll be as quick as possible, ring me if you need to or if you think of anything specific you need.'

'Thanks.'

He found his car in the staff car park, and drove straight to the surgery, even though he was desperate for a shower and a change of clothes. There was a tie in his jacket pocket, and for a moment he contemplated it, but he was in a hurry now. He probably should have gone home, but for some reason he just needed to be here, amongst his friends, and it was nearly eleven, so with any luck the patients would have gone by now so they didn't have to see him looking like this. He walked in, straight up the stairs past a couple of waiting patients and the startled receptionist, ignoring their concerned questions, and into the staffroom.

It was crowded, and they all turned and stared at him, Sam Cavendish getting to his feet and breaking the silence first.

'Nick! How is he?'

'He's...' He couldn't finish, couldn't find the words, and Chloe gasped and covered her mouth with her hand. 'No! He can't be—'

He shook his head. 'No. He's all right,' he said hastily, and there was a collective sigh of relief. 'He's stable now and out of Intensive Care. It's been...um...'

He didn't know what to say, but they were clustered around him, gathered there as if they'd been waiting, and he lifted his head and met their eyes, seeing the love and concern and support there for him, for Kate, and for Jeremiah. And there was only one thing that mattered, one thing he needed to tell them, these people who were his friends, first and foremost, although they might well not be when they knew.

'It's been a bit of a worry, but it looks like he's going to be all right,' he said, and then he added, 'Actually, we're both going to need some help in the next few weeks with cover. There's something you should know, something I'd rather didn't leave this room. Jeremiah's my son.'

If he'd expected a shocked reaction, he didn't get one.

There was no condemnation, no gasps of horror, just acceptance and support.

It turned out that most of them had worked it out—some, like old Doris Trefussis, cleaner, tea-lady and general all-round good egg, years ago. Sam Cavendish knew, certainly, and when everyone had dispersed and left them alone, Sam put a mug of coffee in his hand and sat down at right angles to him, his bad leg stretched out and propped on the other ankle, a mug cradled in his hands and his eyes thoughtful.

'You can do it, you know,' he said, surprising Nick.

He frowned. 'Do what?'

'Be a good father to him. You were more of a father to me in my teens than my own father had ever been, and I know you've been good to my brother in the ten years I was away. And you love the boy. That means more than anything else.'

Nick gave a soft huff of laughter, and smiled tiredly at Sam. He'd been fond of him since he'd been a boy, and he'd been more than happy to take him on at the surgery when he'd come home wounded after a run-in with insurgents in Africa. And he was glad he had, because Sam had ended up back with Gemma, one of their nurses and his childhood sweetheart, and their baby was due any day. 'When did you get to be so wise, Sam?' he asked softly, but Sam just smiled back and ignored his remark.

'We need to sort the rota out, because Gemma can't go on much longer. She's been having contractions off and on for days and every morning I wake up and think, How can she still be pregnant? So it won't be long, and we'll need another locum if you aren't going to be here.'

'Why not? I can still work most of the time.'

'No—because you'll be at your son's bedside,' he offered gently. 'Does he even know yet?'

Nick felt emotion well in his chest and cleared his throat. 'No. We're going to tell him when he's a bit stronger. To be honest, I'm dreading it and I'm happy to put it off as long as possible.'

'Don't leave it too long,' Sam advised, as if he hadn't already done that very thing, then he tilted his head on one side and raised a brow. 'You look like hell, by the way,' he said conversationally, and Nick growled softly under his breath.

'If one more person tells me that today I'm going to—'

'What? Go home and shower? Good idea, Nick. You could do with a seriously close shave, a shirt that's seen an iron in living memory and trousers that haven't got more wrinkles than an elephant's hide.'

He looked down at himself and remembered what he'd looked like less than twenty-four hours ago. How could that be? It seemed a lifetime ago. Nearly had been...

'We'll sort out the rota,' Sam was saying. 'I'm booking myself off now for a fortnight, because Gemma was looking iffy this morning, and I'll make sure they book you off, too, and we'd better have open-ended cover for Kate. I think Chloe might already have organised that, but I'll check. Kate's dog is being looked after, so all you need to worry about is your family. Go on, go and sort yourself out and get back to them. Have you had any sleep at all?'

'I had an hour this morning.'

'You might want to get your head down as well, then.'

He shook his head. 'No time. I can't leave Kate without back-up. Oh, and I'll need Chloe to find some stuff for them both. She's got a key to Kate's place. Kate's house keys were on her car keys, and they got left in it. I expect the police have taken them. I need to follow that up.'

He got to his feet with a sigh, put his mug on the draining board and paused at the door. 'Sam—thanks.'

'What for? I owe you more than I can ever repay, Nick. You go and look after your son, and leave the practice to us. We can manage.'

He laughed. 'Easy for you to say, you're booking yourself out on paternity leave as of now!'

'The others can cope. They love a challenge. Go on, shove off.'

He shoved. Half an hour later, after a rapid shower and a desperately-needed shave, dressed in clean trousers and an open-necked casual shirt and feeling a little more human, he headed back to the hospital, armed with Chloe's love for Kate and Jeremiah, the spare key to her cottage and a bag of toiletries and clothes for each of them, which Chloe had kindly picked up while he had been sorting himself out.

He got back at a little after one-thirty, and found Kate sitting by Jem's bed, her face exhausted.

'How is he?' he asked, putting the bags down by the chair, and she shrugged.

'The same, really. He's in a lot of pain—they've just given him more painkillers, and he's gone to sleep at last. Jess came and sat with me for a while, she's very kind. Oh, and Lucy popped in a little while ago—she's going to come back later when you're here. She sends her love. And Jack's been up again.'

He nodded, his eyes welling up. Lucy had sent her love. And Jack had been back, too, giving up his time to a brother he hadn't known he had. It didn't surprise him. His twins were both kind and generous to a fault, and he was immensely proud of them.

'Have you had lunch?'

She shook her head. 'I didn't like to leave him. Have you?'

'No—but he's asleep now, so why don't we pop down to the café and grab something while the going's good?'

She nodded, and got stiffly to her feet, easing

out the kinks and giving him a wry smile. They told the nurses where they were going, then she fell into step beside him as they headed for the café.

'Oh, it's nice to move. I've been so afraid to make a noise in case I disturbed him.'

He smiled ruefully. 'I'm sorry I was so long, but I had to sort out the fallout at the surgery, and I got sick of everyone telling me I needed a shower. So, do I look better?'

She smiled up at him. 'Just a bit.' Actually, she'd quite liked him with the roguish stubbled look, but it was better to have him back with her— much better. She'd missed him. He'd been gone what felt like ages, and it had been a bit of an emotional roller coaster watching Jem in pain. It was good to step off the ride for a moment now he was comfortably asleep.

Nick looked up at the menu, then glanced at her. 'What are you having?'

'Oh, I don't know. Vegetables! All I've had in the last twenty-four hours is sandwiches. I'm sick of bread.'

'They've got salads.'

'Perfect.'

'I'll get you one. Go and sit down over there by

the window and relax,' he ordered, so she went, and a few moments later he set a laden tray down in front of her.

She tried to summon up some enthusiasm. 'That looks nice,' she lied. 'What do I owe you?'

'Owe me?'

'For my lunch.'

He scowled at her. 'Don't be ridiculous. I got you a fruit smoothie as well as the salad because I know you like them and I thought you were probably sick of tea and coffee, too.'

'I am.' She gave him a tired little smile, all she could manage. 'Thank you, Nick.'

He scowled again. 'Don't keep thanking me. I've made a complete fist of everything I've ever done for you. It's high time I started balancing the books.'

If only. She gave a quiet sigh and picked up her knife and fork, wondering how long she was going to be based at the hospital and when she'd be able to go home and lie down in her own bed, just for an hour or two. She was so tired, so very, very tired…

'Kate?'

She pushed her plate away. 'I'm sorry. I'm not really hungry.'

'You're exhausted. You should be in bed.'

'I can't, Nick. I have to be here for him. Tomorrow. I'll go home tomorrow—maybe in the morning, once we've seen Martin Bradley and we know if he's happy with him. I could go home then and have a rest.'

'OK. But if you're doing that, you're eating your salad now. Come on, you can do it.'

And so, with him coaxing and cajoling her, she finished most of it, drank the smoothie and then realised she was feeling more human. 'You're so sickeningly right always, aren't you?' she said with a smile, and a fleeting frown crossed his face.

'Now I know you need sleep,' he said gruffly, and stabbed his fork into the last slice of tomato on his plate and put it in his mouth.

She laughed at him. 'That's better,' she said softly. 'You sound more like the old Nick.'

He pushed his plate away and thought about it, realising she was right. 'I feel better. It's amazing what a shower and a square meal can do. I've brought you some things, by the way. Chloe sorted them out—she sends her love. Well, everyone at the practice sends their love,' he amended with a smile that felt distinctly crooked. 'I told them he's my son,' he added, his voice low. 'I hope you don't mind. I asked them to keep it quiet.'

'How did they take it?'

He shrugged. 'It was odd. They didn't seem at all surprised. In fact, they were incredibly supportive. Chloe had arranged cover for you for the rest of this week already, but I've told her I'm writing you off sick for four weeks—'

'Four? Why?'

He smiled again, this time a little wryly. 'Because you've got whiplash,' he reminded her.

'No, I haven't.'

'I'm sure you have. You're having four weeks to get over it, whatever,' he told her, and, actually, she found she didn't mind his high-handed approach this time, because she needed the time to devote to Jem, and it wasn't entirely false. Her neck was a little sore.

She rolled it, wincing slightly, and he found himself aching to ease it for her, to massage it gently until it relaxed so she could get some relief. 'Sam's signing off on paternity leave—and, no, Gemma's not in labour, as far as I know, but he wasn't quite sure if she was on the verge this morning so he's booked a locum anyway.'

'She's a week overdue,' Kate said, biting her lip. 'I should be there for her.'

'Don't worry. Chloe's there, she'll look after her. And Sam is a doctor. They should be able to cope without you. And Sam's getting a locum to cover me for the next week at least, unless they really can't manage without me. I want to be here for you both,' he added, when she started to protest.

She said nothing for a moment, then sighed softly. 'Thank you. I don't know how I would have coped without you yesterday and last night.'

'I would have been here anyway, Kate,' he told her quietly. 'Even if he wasn't my son, I would have been here for you.'

She nodded. 'Yes, I know you would. That's the funny thing about you, you're so generous, so kind, so helpful, but if anybody dares to realise it, you get so uncomfortable—look, you're doing it now.'

She shook her head slowly, carefully folding her paper napkin for something to do with her hands, because it would have been so easy to reach out to him, to take the hand lying on the table, fiddling with the little sugar packets.

'We ought to tell Jem, I suppose,' he murmured.

'Nobody in the hospital apart from Jack and Ben knows, so it shouldn't leak out, which means we can tell him when the time's right.'

He carried on fiddling, piling up the sugar packets and pushing them into straight lines with his fingertip. 'I'd just like to do it when I've had a chance to build a relationship with him—made friends with him, got to know him a bit better. You're right, I haven't ever really talked to him, or spent meaningful time with him, and it's time I did. Time I gave him a chance to get to know me, too. And it'll give you a bit of a break as well, if we're sharing the visiting. It's going to be a long haul.'

She nodded. 'Yes. Yes, I know. It should be better once he's on the mend, though. They have lessons and activities and he'll be doing physio, and there will be other kids for him to talk to. And his friends'll be able to visit in a few days' time, so that'll take the heat off us, too.'

And who knew? They might even find some time to be together themselves. That was a novel thought, but probably not one that would lead to anything. She'd do well to keep reminding herself of that fact, because it would be all too easy to fall into the habit of relying on him only to find he wasn't there when it came to the crunch.

She was sure he meant well, and maybe this time he really thought he could do it, but she wasn't holding her breath.

CHAPTER FIVE

MEGAN PHILLIPS, the pretty young paediatric registrar who'd been on call overnight, was waiting for them at the nursing station.

'We've got his blood results,' she began, and Nick felt his heart stall.

Don't let him have a problem. Not thrombocytopenia, he thought. Please don't let it be that, don't let him have DIC.

'He's OK now, but the biochemistry was a bit skewed. We needed to tweak some of the components, but it probably explains why he was feeling a bit rough. We've started an infusion and he should be fine now. We'll check it again in a while, OK?'

Relief hit him like a wall, and he smiled and thanked her, wishing, as a doctor, he didn't know so much. Ignorance would be bliss, he thought as he ushered Kate back into the side room where Jem was still sleeping. She stopped in the doorway and put her hand over her mouth for a second, sucking in air, and he squeezed her shoulder.

'He's all right,' he murmured.

'I know, but he looks so vulnerable, so fragile lying there like that,' she murmured.

'He'll be fine. You heard Megan,' he said firmly, and watched as she perched on the edge of the armchair by the bed.

It was upholstered in a hideous pink—wipe-clean vinyl, of course—and he found himself wondering how many parents had sat on it and watched their children.

He sat on the arm, laid his hand on Kate's shoulder and watched his son sleeping…

Megan reached out her hand to pick up the phone, and it fell back to her lap, nerveless with shock.

No!

It couldn't be him! She'd heard there was an O'Hara starting in A and E, but it had never occurred to her it was him, that he'd be here in Cornwall, of all places! She'd thought she'd be safe here, never have to see him again, never have to be reminded…

Her heart raced, and she shrank back into the chair, trying to get away, retreating from the sight of him. She must be mistaken, she told herself. It wasn't Josh. It couldn't be.

But it was him—tall, lean, more attractive even than he'd been eight years ago. He was the most good-looking man she'd ever seen, so sure of himself, so at home in his own skin that he exuded an almost tangible aura of confident masculinity. Alpha man. A man that women couldn't resist. A man who only had to crook his little finger and stupid, senseless little girls would abandon all their brains and follow him to the end of the earth.

He glanced over and caught sight of her, his body arresting momentarily, then excusing himself he walked towards her, resting a hand on the top of the counter and looking down at her with those extraordinary indigo-blue eyes, and she couldn't look away, for all she wanted to.

'Megan?'

His voice was shocked, his eyes dark with a host of emotions she couldn't even guess at, but it wasn't his emotions she was worried about, it was her own, tumbling in free-fall as she stared back at him, mesmerised, horrified, memory after memory crashing through her and robbing her of speech.

She unglued her tongue from the roof of her mouth and tried to remain professional.

'Hello, Josh.'

Just the two words. It was all she could manage, all she could force out through lips that were stiff with shock.

His hair fell over his forehead, and he threaded his fingers through the glossy black strands and raked it out of the way, making her suck in her breath. She could still remember the soft, silky feel of it between her fingers. 'I didn't know you worked here,' he said, that soft Irish brogue rippling over her nerve-endings like little tongues of flame. 'How are you?'

He looked vaguely stunned, his eyes wary now, concerned. As well they might be after what he'd done...

'I'm—I'm fine. Busy. Excuse me, I need to make a call.'

'That's OK, you can do it in a moment. I'm looking for a patient who's had surgery for a fractured pelvis—Jem Althorp? I put on the ex-fix in A and E.'

'He's fine. There's a minor problem with his bloods, that's all. He's in that room there. Now, I need to deal with this, Josh, and I don't need to deal with you. Excuse me.'

And picking the phone up again with shaking hands, she rang the haematology department, conscious all the while of Josh standing there, until with a quiet sigh he turned on his heel and walked away.

She nearly wept with relief.

The rest of the day dragged for Kate and Nick.

Josh O'Hara had popped in briefly, but he'd seemed distracted and hadn't stayed long. Just long enough for them to thank him for the procedure that might well have saved their son's life.

Jem's blood was quickly sorted, as Megan had promised, and he was feeling better, but by the evening Kate was at the end of her tether, and Nick sent her off to bed at nine, when Jem had drifted off to sleep again.

'I'll sit up with him.'

'But you haven't had any sleep either,' she protested. 'I've had more than you.'

'I haven't been in a car accident,' he said firmly. 'Go on. I'll get you if there's the slightest thing to worry about, but there won't be.'

'But how will you know?' she asked, fretting.

'You don't know him—you don't know how he sleeps, and what's normal—'

'Kate, he's just a child, like any other,' he said gently. 'If he's sick, I'll know. He'll be fine. Go to bed before you drop to pieces.'

So she went, reluctantly, and he settled down in the hateful pink chair and watched the monitor blinking steadily, watched the nice, even trace of Jem's heartbeat through the night, while the staff came in and did hourly obs and brought him endless cups of tea.

And then at three Kate came and took over, sending Nick off to grab some sleep, and he went into the little room where she'd been sleeping and lay down on the still-warm bed, her scent all around him and the residual heat of her body seeping into him like a soothing balm, sending him into a deep, restful sleep.

Jem woke shortly before six, and Kate could see at once that he was stronger.

'Morning, soldier,' she murmured, and, leaning forwards, she stroked his hair back off his forehead and smiled at him. 'How are you?'

'I feel better,' he said. 'I don't hurt so much, and I don't feel so sick. I'm hungry, though.'

He'd graduated from nil by mouth to sips of water, and so Kate poured a little into the beaker and held it to his lips. 'Maybe they'll let you eat something light later on. I've got some wash things for you. You'll feel better after we clean your teeth and wash your face with nice hot water,' she said soothingly. 'Grandma sends her love, and so does Chloe and everyone at the practice.'

'Where's Uncle Nick?' he asked.

She stroked his hair. 'He's here. He spent the night next to you in this chair, and then I got up and swapped over. I expect he's still sleeping. Why?'

He shrugged his skinny shoulders. 'Just wondered. I thought he might have gone home.'

She shook her head. 'No. He wouldn't leave you,' she told him, and she watched something terrifyingly like hero-worship dawn in his eyes.

But all he said was, 'Oh,' and then his eyes drifted shut again and he lay quietly for a while.

Behind her the door opened and closed, and she knew it was Nick without turning round.

'How is he?'

'Awake. Better. He was asking where you were.'

'I'm right here, son,' he said softly, the irony of

it catching her in mid-chest as he perched on the foot of the bed and laid his hand lightly on Jem's ankle 'How are you?'

Jem opened his eyes. 'OK.'

'Good.'

Kate saw Nick's shoulders drop a fraction, and knew he'd been worried. 'He's hungry.'

'That's a good sign,' he said, and his shoulders dropped a little further.

'My bruises hurt,' Jem mumbled from the bed. 'My leg's really sore, and my side hurts, and my elbow's sore, but it's not like it was yesterday.'

'It'll feel better soon.'

There was a tap on the door, and a nurse popped her head round. 'We were going to give Jem a bit of a wash, if you two want to get some breakfast,' she said, and so they went down to the café that was fast becoming their second home, and had bacon rolls and pastries and lashings of coffee.

'One day I'll get home and start eating proper food,' she said, pushing the last crumbs around the plate. 'I never have anything like this for breakfast. I have yogurt and fruit.'

'You could have had yogurt and fruit,' Nick said with a frown, but she just smiled.

'I know, but I wanted a bacon roll, and I couldn't resist the pastries.'

He laughed, and, reaching out his hand, he covered hers and enfolded it in his warm, gentle grasp. 'Crazy woman,' he said, his thumb stroking slow circles over the back of her hand, and she felt the ice inside her starting to thaw, replaced by a strange heat that warmed her from deep inside, somewhere in the region of her heart.

'You need to go home this morning,' he went on gently. 'You're exhausted, and you need a shower and just to get out of here. Once the doctors have been round and they're happy, I'm going to take you home—and don't argue.'

She smiled a little unsteadily. 'I won't. It sounds wonderful. I could really do with a change of scenery, just for a little while. I ought to sort my car out, too, really. I need the keys.'

'We can phone the police, get that organised,' he said. 'I'll contact them. And you'll need another car.'

She rolled her eyes. 'I have no idea how long that'll take.'

'We'll get you one today,' he said. 'What do you want?'

She frowned at him. 'Why should you do that?'

'Because he's my son? Because you need it to transport him? I'll get you a bigger one, a stronger one.'

'No! I'll get it, and, besides, it can't be big, I have to be able to park in tight spaces.'

'So I'll get you a small stronger one.'

She sighed. 'Nick, that other driver must have been going at well over forty. Nothing's that strong. And I need it to do my job as well. Maybe I'll have to get a contract one through the PCT after all.'

'They can't do it that quickly. I can get you a car today—or at least organise it.'

She sighed again. 'Nick, it's very kind of you, but I don't really need it in a tearing hurry if I'm going to be stuck here for days.'

He shrugged. 'So you can have one in days. Just tell me what you want.'

She gave up. Sort of. 'I'll think about it,' she told him, and changed the subject.

The doctors were pleased with him. The blood setback seemed to have been resolved—routine, as Martin Bradley had said—his wound was healing well, and he was happy for them to leave the hospital—for a short while.

'Don't be too long,' Jem said, having a little wobble just as they left, and she hesitated, but Nick's hand on her arm was firm, and she promised they wouldn't be long and let him lead her out.

They went via the police station to pick up her keys and the items that had been in her car, and Nick put the bag in his boot and drove her home. It was the first time she'd been back since the accident, and it felt like for ever. She walked inside, picking up the post as she went, and then looked around.

The place was littered with Jem's things. A book on the stairs, his sports bag in the hall, a jumper dropped on the floor in the sitting room.

It caught her totally unawares, and she stared at the things numbly. What on earth would it have been like to come back to this if he'd died?

'I need a shower—put the kettle on and make yourself a drink,' she said, and hurried upstairs, needing to get away from Nick, to hide herself away in the shower where the sound of water might drown the threatening sobs that were rising in her throat.

She stripped her clothes off, the sobs starting to break free, and stepped into the shower, turning her face to the wall and slumping on it, her hands pressed over her mouth to hold in the pain that had been bottled up for days, the pain she couldn't hold inside any longer.

She could so easily have lost him. Just another couple of miles an hour...

A wrenching sob ripped through her, and she folded over, propping herself up under the pounding spray.

She was crying.

He'd heard the sound before. She'd done the same thing when James had died, and he'd brought her home from the headland and sent her to shower and warm up.

He couldn't go there again—not in the shower with her, holding her—but how could he leave her? How could he have left her then, torn apart by grief?

He went up.

She hadn't locked the bathroom door, and he opened the shower cubicle and turned off the water. She was huddled in the corner, and he reached for a towel and crouched down, draping it round her as he lifted her out, sitting down on the floor with her curled into his lap, her tears giving way slowly to fractured sobs that tore at his heart.

'He could have died,' she said at last, her voice fragmented by emotion. 'I came in and saw all his things, and I thought, What if I'd come back here, like I did when James died, and his things were everywhere—and...'

She broke off, fisting her hands in his shirt, and he held her closer, rocking her gently, hot tears scalding his eyes again as she clung to him, sobbing. 'Shh. He's all right, Kate, he's getting better now. He's going to be all right, sweetheart, he really is. You have to believe that.'

She nodded and sniffed, the sobs dying away to random hiccups. Every now and then there was another little bout, but he just held her close and let her cry, let her get it out of her system until at last she lifted her head and let go of his shirt, then swiped the tears from her face with shaking fingers.

'I'm sorry.'

'Don't be.'

'I always do this, don't I? Hide in the shower to cry.'

He shushed her again, smoothing the damp strands of hair back from her face and pressing his lips softly to her tear-stained cheek.

'All right now?'

She nodded slowly, and he eased her out of her arms, rescuing the towel as it slid down and tucking it back round her.

'I'll leave you to wash. I'll be downstairs,' he told her, and, standing up, he pulled her to her feet and kissed her cheek again. 'I'll make you a cup of tea.'

'Thanks.'

She came down a few minutes later just as the kettle boiled, dressed in clean clothes, her hair still damp and combed out over her shoulders and her smile wry.

'Sorry about that,' she said, looking a little sheepish. 'I just lost it.'

'Don't apologise, you've had a hell of a couple of days. You needed to get it off your chest. And talking of which, I'm a little underdressed. There's a bag of clean clothes in my car that I keep there for emergencies—could you do the honours while I shower? Since I'm already drenched?'

He'd taken off his sodden, crumpled shirt, but the trousers clung to his legs and her eyes scanned his body. Comparing him to Rob? He wouldn't come off well. He took care of himself, but Rob was a fitness fanatic and a PE teacher. And an ex, he reminded himself, and took small comfort from that.

'Sure,' she said, and took the keys, and he went upstairs to the bathroom. When he emerged from the shower a few moments later, the bag was there, just inside the door, with a clean, dry towel. She'd come in, and he hadn't noticed. Just as well, he decided, because when that towel had slipped he'd had a whole plethora of inappropriate thoughts and frankly he wouldn't trust himself with her at the moment.

He went back downstairs and found her sitting at the kitchen table with a cup of tea, and she ran her eyes over him again and smiled.

'It's a good job you keep spare clothes in your car,' she said, pushing a mug of tea towards him, and he gave a rueful laugh and sat down.

'Well, more or less. Trousers and shirt, at least, for predictable accidents. I don't tend to carry underwear.'

She chuckled, then sat back and eyed him thoughtfully. 'Are you telling me you're going commando, Dr T.?' she asked softly, raising an eyebrow and trying to stop her mouth from twitching, and the inappropriate thoughts leapt into his head again.

'That depends who wants to know,' he murmured, feeling the smile tug his own mouth, and the twitch got worse.

'Are you flirting with me?'

He felt his smile fade and searched her beautiful, teasing brown eyes. 'Would that be such a bad thing?' he asked softly.

The teasing look vanished, and there was a moment of breathless silence. 'I don't know— would it?'

'I'm not sure. It might be fun. It would make a change—we haven't had fun like that since our teens.' He glanced down at the mug, lined the handle up carefully exactly at right angles and then met her eyes. 'How about it?'

'How about what?' she asked carefully, and he thought she was holding her breath.

'Us.'

'I'm not sure that would be a good idea,' she said, after a seemingly endless pause. 'Maybe we'd just better concentrate on Jem for now.'

She'd hesitated, and in that time he'd held his

own breath. He let it out now and gave a little shrug. 'If you want.'

'I want. Things are complicated enough.'

He nodded, and she gave a quiet sigh of relief. She didn't want to rush into anything. There was, however, another worry that was playing on her mind, a more immediate problem, and she raised it now.

'Nick, how am I going to manage when he comes out of hospital? I don't have a downstairs bathroom, or even a cloakroom, and stairs could be really difficult at first.'

'You could come to mine.'

She shook her head instantly. 'No. Not to Annabel's house,' she said softly, and watched the guilt flash across his eyes before he looked away.

'No. You're right, it wouldn't feel appropriate and, anyway, it's not exactly off the beaten track. So—perhaps we could rent somewhere? A bungalow or something, neutral ground. Just for a while, until he can manage the stairs again. I'm sure there are things out there. It's only April. It might be harder in August with the tourists, but I'm sure we could find something now and it needn't be for long. A few weeks, maybe.'

A rental property? 'It's worth a try,' she said, feeling the weight of that worry lifting from her shoulders with relief. 'I would never have thought of that.'

His smile was a little crooked. 'You see? I can have my uses, slight though they might be. I'll call the agents now.'

He made a couple of calls while she dried her hair, and when she came down he was fizzing with suppressed excitement.

'There's a single-storey barn conversion. They've been trying to sell it, but it hasn't gone because it's quite pricy and the owners have been unrealistic, but they've now decided to let it, but only to people who don't want a long lease, which we don't.'

She nodded slowly. 'OK. Where is it?'

'On the way to Ben and Lucy's, so only about three miles out of the village. It's got a distant sea view, apparently—it's U-shaped, two-storey in the central section, with a courtyard garden and surrounded by farmland. Worth a look?'

'Definitely,' she said, then hesitated, not sure how to ask but just knowing that she had to, that this needed to be set out in black and white.

'Nick—is this just for me to stay in, or were you thinking of being there, too?'

He gave an enigmatic shrug, his eyes veiled. 'That depends.'

'On?'

'You, Jem? I don't know. If you want me there, I'd like to be there, but I don't want to confuse him or pre-empt any decision you might make in the future. I know Rob lived with you, but—'

'No,' she corrected hastily. 'Rob didn't live with us. He and Matt came to stay after I came out of hospital, but the boys shared Jem's room and Rob was on the sofa bed downstairs. We didn't share a room. It didn't feel right, when it came to it.'

He wasn't sure why, but that made him feel better. Not much. He knew they'd had an intimate relationship, because he'd gone to talk to her one night about a year ago and seen them through the window. He could still picture Rob bending his head to kiss her in the kitchen, and then the lights going off and coming on upstairs. Not that there was any reason why they shouldn't, but that had been before her surgery. Maybe that had changed things. Was that what she had meant about it not feeling right?

'I don't have any ulterior motive, Kate,' he told

her. 'There are four bedrooms there. Two upstairs, each with en suite, and an en suite guest room, another bedroom or snug and a study downstairs in one of the sides. It's got a big open living space with a sitting room one end, a kitchen at the other and an open vaulted dining hall in the middle, with the stairs off it, and the third side is utility, workshop and garaging, apparently. We'd have plenty of space.'

She blinked. 'It sounds amazing.'

'That's what I thought. I've asked the agent to meet us there in twenty minutes.'

Her eyes widened. 'Wow. OK. You don't hang around, do you?'

'Is that a problem?'

'No. No, no problem, it's been worrying me to bits. It would be great if it was any good. The only thing is, how much is the rent, because I can't afford a fortune.'

'You let me worry about that.'

'Nick, I can't—'

'You can. It's not for you, it's for our son, and God knows I've done precious little for him in the last eleven years. Just let it go, Kate. Please. Don't argue.'

She opened her mouth, thought for a moment

and then gave in. 'OK. But don't get in the habit of doing this.'

'What? Caring for my son? Why the hell not?'

There was a look in his eyes she hadn't seen for years, a purpose, a passion, and it was as if this whole course of events had brought him back to life.

She smiled. 'Shall we go and look?' she said, and he grinned and tossed his car keys in the air.

'After we've been via mine and I've got some underwear on,' he said with a mischievous twinkle that gave her heart an unexpected lurch, and he ushered her out, closing the door firmly behind them.

It was fantastic. Perfect.

Built of granite, it was solid, tucked down in a fold of the land to shelter it from the prevailing south-westerly wind, and he couldn't find a single thing wrong with it.

It was to let fully furnished with every necessity and equipped to a very high standard, with king-size beds in the main bedrooms, lovely battered leather sofas in the sitting room and invitingly luxurious bathrooms with showerheads like dustbin lids.

He hadn't felt so excited about anything for years. He'd made his mind up after the most cursory walk-through and an exchanged glance with Kate, who was looking slightly stunned. It was wonderful, and he couldn't imagine why it hadn't sold instantly.

He said as much to the agent, who just shrugged. 'I don't know, either. It's been a second home and their circumstances have changed and they want to sell it, but they want a lot for it. The only thing I can assume is that it's too expensive for a holiday cottage and there aren't enough people living around here who can afford to buy it. As far as I can see, there isn't a single catch apart from the price, but the market's been a little odd recently. Maybe that's it.'

Maybe. And it was expensive, but Nick was doing some quick calculations. He wasn't a big spender. He'd been careful over the years, he was sitting on the cash he'd got for his parents' house when Ben had bought it at auction for Lucy, and if he sold his own house, he'd have enough to buy it.

Not that he was going to do anything rash just

yet, but it might be worth having a word with the agent to see if he could have the option on it as they were renting. And maybe, if things went well…

'What do you think, Kate?'

Her smile was enigmatic. 'I think we need to talk.'

He frowned, as if he couldn't see what on earth they might need to talk about, and then with a slight shrug he turned to the agent.

'Can we have another wander around for a few minutes, talk this through?' he asked, and the agent nodded.

'Sure. Take your time. I've got a few calls to make, I'll be in the car.'

He left them, and Nick turned to Kate.

'Well? Come on, let's hear it, you've obviously got something you want to say.'

She smiled at his impatience, but she wasn't going to be railroaded, no matter what she thought of the house. 'I think it's wonderful,' she told him honestly. 'Absolutely gorgeous. I also think it'd be impossible going from this back to my house when he's better.'

He gave her a level look. 'Maybe you won't have to.'

'Because I'll sell up and move away?'

'I wasn't thinking of that. I was thinking you might stay on, live here.'

'Nick...' She gave a little, despairing laugh and shook her head. 'We can't just live here for ever.'

'Why not?'

She felt her eyes widen. 'Why not? Because it's outrageously expensive! I can't even afford to rent it, let alone buy it—'

'But I can. I could buy it, and you could stay here.'

'No.' She backed away from him a step, shaking her head again but in denial this time. 'Nick, no. Don't try and buy me, please. Or Jem. Especially not him. I'd rather carry him up and downstairs or put his bed in the sitting room with a commode beside it than let you do that. Please. I mean it.'

He sighed and rammed his hand through his hair. 'Kate, I'm not trying to buy you, don't be silly. I'm just talking through the possibilities.'

'Well, how about possibly finding a simple, small bungalow somewhere with three bedrooms while he recovers?' she suggested bluntly, not sure she could picture him in that setting but pushing him just to see if he'd go for it, for his son's sake. For hers.

He stabbed his hand through his hair again and gave an exasperated sigh. 'Look, forget the money, forget the value, because it's not about that, it's not about impressing you, or Jem. It's about giving us somewhere to get to know each other, all of us, somewhere calm and safe, tranquil, somewhere we can all heal, because I'm under no illusions about it. When we tell him I'm his father there will be some wounds that need healing, Kate, and we'll need somewhere to do that in peace.'

He was so right—of course. He took her hands, meeting her searching gaze with troubled eyes, eyes that were filled with sincerity and pain. 'That's why I've held back, Kate, why I haven't involved myself with Jem, not because I didn't want to rock the boat with my other kids, but because of what it would do to him. I thought, when there was a possibility that you'd marry Rob, that he might not ever need to know, that he could have a stepfather who'd love him and keep him safe, and the knowledge that his father had died a hero. But now you aren't going to marry Rob, and it was only with the blood group thing that I realised there was no question that he was mine, and that he had to know.'

He dropped her hands and turned to the window, gesturing at the courtyard garden. 'Look at it, Kate. It's warm, sheltered, with flat paths where he can walk safely while he heals. Your garden's terraced at the back, your drive slopes up to the house and there are steps to the front door. My garden's the same, and it's so public there—so many people who'd make it their business to have an opinion and to express it. If I'm ten minutes late taking the milk in, there's someone there with it in their hand, ringing the bell and checking up on me.'

'And you don't want people to see us together? Is that it?' she asked, a hideous sinking feeling in her chest. 'Are you ashamed of him, Nick? Because if you are, this stops now. I'm not having my son thinking you're ashamed of him—'

'Kate, no!' he exclaimed, his face horrified, and she knew instantly that he wasn't lying. 'Of course I'm not ashamed of him! I think he's a great kid—and I'm really proud to be his father. I just dread the impact it'll have on him when it gets out, and if there was anything I could do to protect him from that, to prevent it happening,

I would do it, believe me, but I can't. I can just be there for him, to fend off the gossips, and the easiest way to do that is to avoid them. At least here we'd be free to explore our relationship in peace, and can you think of a better place to do it?'

He was right, of course, but even though she was reassured about his motives, she still had doubts.

'I don't want him to know you're thinking of buying it, Nick,' she said slowly. 'Not at first.'

He lifted his hands in a shrug. 'Why not? I'm still his father, I still intend to be part of his life, and maybe it's time to move on from the home I shared with Annabel. He can come and stay here with me. And if you move away, he'll be staying for longer—weekends, weeks…' He broke off and rammed his hands in his pockets.

'I don't know if I am,' she said slowly. 'Moving away.'

His eyes narrowed. 'I thought you'd handed in your notice to the PCT?'

'Not yet. I didn't get round to posting it. And now—well, now, maybe I should stay. That depends on you, on your relationship with Jem, on how you get on once he knows you're his father. We'll have to see.'

'But—'

'Nick, don't push it,' she warned, too emotionally fraught to make sensible decisions about their future right then. 'I need time to think this through, and I don't want to feel under pressure.'

'I know. And I want to give you that time. Please don't feel pressured, Kate. I don't want to do that. I'm just trying to give you all the options, and this might be one of them, if you think you'd like it to be.'

'You obviously would,' she murmured, watching his face, and he turned and gave her a crooked little smile.

'I would. I love it here. The moment I stepped inside, I felt it wrap itself around me. I know it sounds crazy, Kate, but I felt as if I'd come home, for the first time in my adult life. And I want it—the whole package. All of it.'

The whole package? Did he mean them, too? Or was she reading things into his words that didn't exist? Whatever he meant, when she searched his eyes she found nothing but a burning sincerity. For all his flaws, Nick Tremayne was nothing if not honest and honourable, and she knew he was only telling her the truth. If he said he'd give her time and not pressure her, he meant it. Whatever his ulterior motives.

And so she nodded. 'OK. We'll try. We'll tell Jem it's just rented, that it's only till he's better, so there are no carrots dangling in front of him, nothing to influence him in any way, and we'll see how it goes. All right?'

His mouth quirked into a wry smile, and he nodded.

'Sure. Sounds good. Let's go and tell the agent he's got a deal,' he said, and she followed him, wondering if it would work, hoping that it would and that it wouldn't all turn out to be the most hideous mistake…

CHAPTER SIX

THEY shook hands on the deal, agreed they could take possession of it as early as the next day and went back to the hospital, Nick still with that air of suppressed excitement about him, Kate assailed by doubts.

Their track record wasn't great. What if this was just another disaster in the making?

Think positive! she told herself, and walked with him up to the ward.

They found Lucy at her new-found brother's bedside, Jem propped up a little, a games console in his hand and an intent expression on his face. Lucy looked up at them with a smile. 'Hi.'

'Hi. Everything all right?'

'Fine.'

'OK, I'll see you in a few minutes, I've got some calls to make,' Nick said, and headed for the door. 'I won't be long.'

Kate perched on the chair by the bed and leant over towards Jem. 'So what's this?'

He grinned at her. 'Lucy's lent it to me—it's Ben's, and it's really cool. And I made her cry.'

Lucy looked a little sheepish. 'He was so sweet—he said he'd wanted one for ages, and it just got to me.'

'Oh, Lucy.'

She shrugged, smiled and carried on watching him as he got to grips with it, and moments later Nick came back in and sat on the chair beside her, perching on the arm with his hip against her side and the subtle scent of his cologne drifting over her, carried on the warmth of his body.

She thought of sharing the barn with him, and a little shiver of anticipation swept over her skin.

'So what's that?' he asked, and she looked up at him and smiled.

'Lucy brought him in a games console,' she said softly. 'He was so thrilled, he made her cry. He's wanted one for ages and we just haven't been able to afford it.'

Jem caught sight of Nick then and grinned excitedly. 'Hey, look what Lucy's lent me, Uncle Nick,' he said.

'I'm looking,' he said, deeply touched that his son wanted to share his excitement, but—Uncle Nick? 'That looks cool.'

'It's not just cool—it's awesome,' he said, stretching the word and making Nick's lips twitch. 'Absolutely epic! Lucy's lent it to me. You can do all sorts of things with it.'

'That's kind of you, Lucy,' Nick said, feeling a little choked and also inadequate because he'd been in such a hurry to get back yesterday he hadn't brought him in anything, and today he'd been so preoccupied with the barn that a simple thing like a present for his child hadn't even entered his head.

Lucy tutted. 'Don't be silly, Dad—it was lying around at home and we hardly ever use it, but don't imagine you're keeping it, half-pint, because it won't happen.'

She ruffled his hair gently, and he grinned and ducked slightly out of her way as she bent to kiss him, but she followed him and blew a raspberry on his forehead and made him laugh and grimace.

'You be good, and no giving the nurses trouble, or I'll set Ben on you, OK?'

'OK,' he agreed, and smiled at her a little shyly. 'Thank you for bringing it in. It's really nice of you.'

'My pleasure. You take care. I'll see you soon.'

She hesitated by Nick, and then, going up on tiptoe, she kissed his cheek. 'Bye, Dad. I'll see you later. We need to talk,' she added, and he gave a brief nod.

'Yes, we do. Soon. Bye, Lucy. And thank you.'

'I want to try the face thing later,' Jem said as she went out. 'It's got a really cool thing where you can take pictures of people and it shows how they're the same, like eyes and stuff. And Lucy says you look like Jack, so we're going to try it when he comes to see me again.'

Nick swallowed. It wasn't only he and Jack that looked alike, he realised now that he was able to admit it, and Lucy had obviously thought of that, too. 'That sounds really interesting, I'll have to have a look at it some time. You seem much better,' he added, quickly changing the subject and relieved that he was sounding so much perkier, even though he could see he was beginning to flag now Lucy had gone.

'It doesn't hurt so much any more. They gave me some stronger painkillers just before Lucy came. My leg still aches a lot, though.'

'I'm not surprised. It got thumped pretty hard.'

'Is the car completely trashed?' he asked Nick.

'I don't know. I haven't seen it.'

Kate thought of the state it had been in by the time they'd cut the roof and the doors and the front wing off.

'Completely,' she said, shuddering inwardly. 'The boot was full of stuff, and it all got wet when they cut the roof off.' She laughed and felt herself colour. 'The boot's always full of stuff, but I'd sorted out all kinds of things for the charity shop, and I hadn't got round to dropping them off. And it'll be getting mouldy, it's still in the back of your car in a bag, Nick. I ought to deal with it.'

'Don't worry,' he told her, wondering how she could get worked up about something so incredibly trivial in the face of her son's injuries. Or maybe it was because it was trivial that it was safe to worry about it. Safer than thinking about Jem? 'We can sort it out tomorrow.'

She smiled at him and agreed, and then looked at her watch.

'Have you had lunch, Jem?'

'Yes, there was shepherd's pie and peas and jelly and ice cream, but I could only have toast and jelly and ice cream, but I'm having pasta bake tomorrow 'cos I can eat properly then, they said. The jelly and ice cream was nice, though.'

'Good, I'm glad. And it's good news you can eat properly tomorrow, but you should be resting now. Why don't we leave you to sleep, and Uncle Nick and I—'

She broke off, hesitating over the Uncle Nick thing, and looked at him in mute distress, but he just smiled and said, 'We'll go and grab some food while you have a bit of a zizz, and we'll be back. OK, Jem?'

'OK,' he said, and he held the game out to Kate, his eyelids drooping. 'Can you stick that in my locker so it's safe? I don't want it to fall on the floor. I promised Lucy I'd look after it.'

'Sure. Sleep well,' she murmured, and bent over and brushed her lips over his forehead, her stumble over Nick's name reminding her all too forcibly of the conversation that was to come.

'I don't care if you both still call me Uncle Nick,' he said quietly as they walked down to the cafe. 'I don't care what he calls me. It's not what matters.'

Kate felt a little stab of pain for him. 'I know.

I'm sorry, it's just—you've been Uncle Nick for years, and—'

'Kate, it's all right,' he said, squeezing her fingers with his free hand. 'I don't need to be anything else. I was happy being a surrogate uncle, and if that's what he wants when we've told him, I'll carry on. All I ask is the chance to be part of his life.'

'You are part of his life, Nick. You always have been, I've made sure of it. And you always will be.'

She heard him sigh softly, and paused on the stairs, her hand on his arm. 'Nick, it'll be all right. We'll get there.'

'Will we?' he asked doubtfully. 'I hope you're right, Kate, because I've suddenly realised how much I want it, and the thought of losing it all now is untenable.'

The day dragged slowly by.

Jem slept for most of it, still not allowed any visitors apart from family, and Jack and Ben came in turn during the afternoon, when they had a moment.

He was sleeping when Jack arrived, and Kate excused herself for a moment and left the men to talk. God knows, they had enough to say to each other, she thought.

'I'll be back in a few minutes, I just want to make a few phone calls,' she said, and slipped out of the door, pulling it ßbehind her.

Jack met his father's eyes, his own guarded, and Nick sighed quietly. It had taken him a while to rebuild his relationship with Jack once he'd returned to Cornwall, and he was desperately sad that it now seemed in peril again.

'Jack, I—'

'I'm not stopping. I've just come to tell you we want to see you. Tonight, Lucy's house, eight o'clock. Be there—and no excuses.'

And without giving him a chance to argue, he walked out, and Nick sat down heavily on the awful pink vinyl armchair beside the bed and stared unseeingly at his son's face until Kate came back.

'He didn't stay long.'

'Long enough to say what he came for. I've been summoned,' he told Kate softly, standing up again and giving her the chair. 'Eight o'clock tonight, Lucy's. Will you be all right if I leave you to go there?'

She smiled sadly. 'Of course I'll be all right.

I've just heard Gemma's been admitted. I might take a walk up there and see how she's doing. You go and see them, Nick, and try and build some bridges.'

He nodded, wondering how he could be in two places at once and only really wanting to be here, by this injured child he was beginning to realise he loved more than life itself...

Ben came by on his way home after his shift finished, by which time Jem had woken up in pain again.

'I've got the most amazing bruises,' he told Ben, but although he was trying to sound as if he was showing off, Kate could tell he was frightened by them, and she wasn't surprised. When he turned back the blankets and showed his side to Ben, she winced yet again, the sight making her curl up inside.

'That's impressive. I'm not surprised you're hurting. I'll go and find someone.'

He went out, coming back a few moments later with Megan Phillips. They consulted the chart together, and she chatted to Jem about his pain, and then she turned to Kate.

'We want to get the pain under control because

we don't like him hurting, but also because we'd like to get him up soon. We might start sitting him up on the side of the bed tomorrow and see how it goes, and if he tolerates that we'll move to the chair, and so on. It'll be slow, but you'll be in control of what you can manage, Jem. We'll let you guide us. And Mr Bradley wants your physio to start properly from tomorrow, so all your muscles don't forget how to work, but very gently at first, so nothing to worry about. Anyway, I'll talk to you in the morning, and I'm on all night if you're worried about anything, Mrs Althorp. Just get them to call me.'

'Thank you,' she said, smiling at the lovely young woman, her dark hair held back in a clip out of the way, the thick curls trying hard to escape. She was kindness itself, but there was something lurking in the back of her eyes today, Kate thought, that hadn't been there yesterday. Something sad and desperate and a little lost. Her heart went out to her.

'I'll go and update your notes right now, Jem, and get someone to come and give you the extra pain relief shortly, OK? And if you're still really uncomfortable, press the bell and they'll get me and we'll have another look at things.'

'Thanks,' he said, looking relieved, and after she'd gone out he looked up at Ben again. 'Thanks for asking her, Ben.'

'Any time. Right, I'd better go home. Apparently I'm cooking tonight. I'll see you later, Nick?'

'Yes. I'll be there.'

Ben gave him a fleeting smile, murmured, 'Don't worry,' and left them alone with their son.

'Here you go, my gorgeous—jelly and ice cream,' a nurse said, putting it down on his bed table with a smile and helping him sit up a little.

Nick glanced at his watch, and realised it was suppertime. He looked at Kate. 'Why don't you go and have a rest for an hour or so while I sit here with Jem?' he suggested gently. 'Or you could go and get something to eat, as I'm eating at Lucy's.'

For a moment he thought she was going to argue, but then she smiled slightly and went out, and he settled himself on the edge of the pink chair and looked at the instructions for the games console while Jem ate the jelly and ice cream and told him how to work it.

'I don't know how you guys work these things

out,' Nick said, frowning at it, and Jem laughed and took it from him.

'It's easy, Uncle Nick, but don't worry, Rob couldn't work out how to use Matt's, either. It's because you're too old for this kind of thing,' he explained innocently.

'Is that right?' he asked, taking the machine back and having another go. So Rob couldn't work it? He ignored the voice that mocked him for his childish urge to be better than the other man, and got Jem to show him once again. And finally, finally, he cracked it.

After that, dealing with Lucy and Jack didn't seem nearly so daunting…

He left Jem's bedside at seven-thirty, just after Kate came back to sit with him. She'd had a rest, and something to eat, and she looked more like herself.

'I'll come back later and update you,' he promised. 'And I could stay, if you like—take turns, like we did last night.'

'We'll see. Have a lovely time,' she said, but her eyes were saying, Good luck, and he gave her a fleeting smile and left.

It took fifteen minutes to get there, and he

parked the car outside and went in through the kitchen door, the way he'd always gone into his family home. He braced himself for the reception committee, but it was only Ben in the kitchen and he greeted him with a smile and a glass of wine. 'Here—I thought you might need this.'

'I'm driving.'

'Not for a while, and it's only a small glass. They're in the sitting room, go on through. And, Nick? Don't worry. They aren't going to skin you, they just want to understand.'

He nodded, and, taking the wine with him, he walked through the familiar house, feeling like a condemned man going to the gallows. Crazy, because in many ways this was none of their business, it was between him and Kate and Jem, and the only other person he owed an explanation to was Annabel, and she was dead.

But he supposed they felt they were acting as her representatives, and of course there were financial implications. Jeremiah, as his son, was entitled to an equal share of his estate, so each of them would lose a percentage of their stake. Maybe that was what they wanted to discuss. Although he doubted it. His children weren't like that.

Shaking his head slowly, he straightened his

shoulders and went through into the sitting room, and the conversation stopped dead.

'Well, don't mind me,' he murmured, and Lucy coloured.

Not Jack. He stood up, looked his father in the eye and said, 'You'd better sit down. We've got Ed on the webcam.'

He nodded, glad that he'd be able to talk to his other son at last, and sat down opposite the laptop on the coffee table, with Jack and Lucy across from him, visible over the top. So he could see them all, and they could all see him. It was like an interview panel, he thought. Or a jury.

I swear by Almighty God…

'Dad.'

He glanced down at Edward, his face moving a little jerkily but still very recognisable.

'I've been trying to ring you,' Nick told him.

'I know. I didn't answer because I don't know what to say to you,' Ed told him, his voice puzzled and hurt. 'I can't believe it—what the hell were you thinking of?'

Nick sighed and ran a hand through his hair. 'There's nothing I can say or do to change what happened, and I'm not going to make excuses,' he told them all, 'but I meant my vows to your mother, Edward, and I swear it was the only time.'

I swear by Almighty God…

'It's not that. That's between the two of you. I just hope she never knew. It's him I'm thinking about, a boy who thought for years that his father was dead when you could have been taking an active role in his life. Sure, it would have hurt Mum, but we were grown up, it was none of our business, and we could have spent time with him and made him feel wanted. That's what's so gutting, that he didn't have any brothers or sisters there for him when we could have been, so easily.'

Nick shook his head. 'I didn't know. It was Kate's decision not to tell me, and she made it for good reasons. Wrong ones, maybe, but still out of consideration for everyone involved, and there weren't any right ones—'

'Don't palm it off on Kate. You've known for two years,' Jack retorted, cutting in. 'That's two lost years he could have had a father. You should have said something sooner, Dad.'

'How?' he asked. 'And when? She was with someone all last year, and she's been ill. You know that. She's had breast cancer. We could hardly tell him then, could we, with his life in turmoil and another man there ready and willing to act as his father? And before then, well, I guess I was still coming to terms with it—still in denial. I'm sorry you're so angry with us, but the only person I can worry about at the moment is your little brother, and I'm afraid he's taking all my time and thoughts right now.'

Edward frowned. 'How did he take it?'

'He doesn't know yet. He's still in a lot of pain. We're going to tell him later, when he's stronger, and when we've had some time to get to know each other. I'm hoping that with time we'll be able to get to know each other better and he'll learn to forgive us both, but I'm going to be part of his life now, come hell or high water, so I'm glad you've all accepted that, at least.'

'Don't worry about us. We're big enough and ugly enough to take care of ourselves. It's Jem we're all worried about.'

He pinched the bridge of his nose, pressing his thumb and forefinger against his eyes before dragging his hand down his face. 'Who the hell do you think I'm worried about?' he asked hoarsely, scanning all their faces. 'At the end of the day, I've done my bit for you lot. I haven't even started with him. I owe him so much I don't know where to begin—'

'That's what we want to talk to you about. You need to change your will, to make provision for him,' Lucy said, and he glanced across at her and wondered if this had been her idea, his little girl, his peacemaker.

'I already have,' he said quietly. 'I did it yesterday, as soon as I found out—as soon as I was sure. The amendment to the will is with my solicitors in St Piran waiting for my signature.'

'And what about his schooling? We all went to private school. Where will he go?'

'Wherever he wants, Jack. I would think the high school in Penhally, with his friends. I don't want to change his life, I don't have the right to interfere.'

Jack snorted, and he met the condemnation in his eyes with new understanding.

'Is that how you saw my involvement in your lives? As interference?'

'Somewhat,' Edward said bluntly. 'It was "My way or the highway". No middle line, no grey areas, just black or white.'

Nick frowned. 'That's not how I see it at all. I did my best to be a good husband and father.

I gave you guidelines. I thought that was what being a father was, but this—I don't know how to deal with this, how to be a father to him now.'

'Is that why you haven't?'

He looked at her and let his breath out on a long, ragged sigh. 'Yes. Yes, that's exactly why. I want to be a good father to him, to all of you, but I just—I can't seem to do it right, apparently. And with Jem—I didn't even get the chance until recently, and it was so nearly too late…'

He broke off, squeezing his eyes shut, pinching the bridge of his nose again, determined to hold it all together in front of them, but it was all still so raw, the image of Jem lying there in Resus while they cut his clothes away and poured fluids into him etched on his memory in acid.

'I still don't understand how you ended up sleeping with Kate when you were married,' Jack said, sounding so like him that at any other time it might have been funny. 'All the morals you rammed down our throats as kids, and yet you could do that—and you ended up with a child you won't even acknowledge! It's just so damned unfair. At least we knew you loved us—and we thought you loved our mother.'

'I did—and I love Jeremiah,' he told them

earnestly. 'Don't imagine for a moment that I don't, and I fully intend to show him that, given a chance.'

'You're changing the subject,' Jack said. 'I want to know how the hell you came to have a random one-night stand with another woman totally out of the blue!'

'I don't think that's any of your business,' he began, but then he sighed and sat back, giving up the unequal struggle. If he ever hoped to make them understand, he had to explain at least some of it. He looked up and scanned their faces in turn.

'You want to know? All right, I'll tell you.'

'Dad, you don't have to,' Lucy protested, but he shook his head.

'I think I do—because it wasn't totally out of the blue at all. Kate and I go back thirty-five years.'

'We know you dated her.'

He smiled gently at Lucy. 'It was rather more than that. I'd know her since I was fourteen, but I was seventeen when I first really became aware of her; she was only fifteen, though, so we took things slowly—walks up on the moors, swimming, surfing, going for picnics. We went to the cinema, I took her to a rock concert—all pretty innocent stuff. And we fell in love.'

He hesitated, remembering those halcyon days, and then he sucked in a breath and carried on. 'I was in my last year at school, and I'd got into med school in London. We talked about me going away, and I promised I'd come back for her. She was sixteen by then, I was eighteen, and although we still weren't sleeping together, that was pretty much a technicality. By the end of that last summer, I knew Kate's body as well as I knew my own, and I cherished it. But I was going away, and people change, and I didn't want to do anything that might hurt her later, so we held back from that last step. And then I met a girl during Freshers' Week, a beautiful girl with stunning blonde hair and the most incredible blue eyes, while we were being dragged round on some crazy pub crawl in fancy dress, and somehow we ended up in her room. I woke up in the morning feeling sick and ashamed and appalled at what I'd done, but it was too late. She came to me a few weeks later in floods of tears and told me she was pregnant, and I didn't know what to do. I just knew I had no choice but to ask her to marry me, and to make it work.'

'And Kate?' Lucy asked softly. 'What happened about Kate?'

'I came down and saw her, and for the first time ever I lied to her. I told her I'd met someone else and fallen in love, and I was going to marry her. I told her she was pregnant—and Kate was devastated. So was I, because I loved her so much—I never had to explain anything to her, I still don't. She still understands me as no one else ever has, anticipates me, and somehow forgives me. She actually sent us a card, saying she hoped we'd be very happy together. And I did everything I could to be fair to Annabel, to be good to her, because it wasn't her fault I'd got her in that mess, and she was lovely. It was no hardship being married to her, and if I didn't think about Kate, it was OK. But even though I did everything I could to make it feel right, I couldn't, not entirely, because my heart was with Kate and always has been. And even though I was with your mother, I always knew what was going on in Kate's life—we went to her wedding to James, we saw them socially from time to time, and I managed to convince myself that we'd both moved on. Only I never really did, of course, and I don't think she did.'

He tried to smile at them, but his mouth felt

frozen. 'I don't know that I can explain what happened that night—the night of the storm. It was a few hours after my father and your Uncle Phil had died, and Kate's husband had been washed out to sea.'

He filled in the details of the day, the rescue that had gone wrong and led to the death of three men, the horror of it. 'Later that night your mother told me to find Kate, to see if he'd been found, and he hadn't. She was still on the cliff-top, so I took her home and tried to look after her, but she was falling apart, devastated, and so was I, and we just reached out to each other. We've never needed words, and we didn't need them that night. We just hung on while the storm raged all around us, and afterwards I put her to bed and left her, and went back to your mother and tried to carry on.

'And that's what I've done for the past twelve years,' he said, 'tried to carry on, to keep going, keep putting one foot in front of the other and not hurt too many people along the way. And then I find I have another child, a son, and we're going to have to tell him, and yet again I'm going to hurt someone I love.'

He stopped, unsure what else, if anything, he

could tell them, but there was nothing more of any relevance, so with a long, deep breath, he sat back and waited.

He'd told them things he'd never told anyone, not even Kate, and there was a long silence until Lucy knelt up beside him, put her arms round him and rested her head on his shoulder. 'Dad, I'm so sorry,' she whispered, and he could feel a wet patch forming on his shirt from her soundless tears.

He hugged her back, and she dragged in a shuddering breath and sat up. 'Ed, are you OK?' she asked.

Nick looked at Edward, clearly moved even on the jerky picture.

'I'm sorry,' he said. 'We had no right to make you go through that. You were right, it was none of our damn business. Look, I'm going to go. Just—look after him, could you, and send him my love? I'll write to him. You can give him the letter when you think he's ready.'

'Thanks.'

The screen went blank, and Lucy shut the laptop and leant back with a sigh, and he glanced across and saw Jack, stony-faced and silent, but he was far from unmoved, however tight his control.

'Well—I suppose we ought to eat,' Lucy said at last, and, unfolding her legs, she got off the sofa and went out. Seconds later, they heard her crying, and Ben's voice murmuring quietly as he soothed her.

'I'm sorry, I probably shouldn't have told you all of that,' Nick said softly, but Jack made a dismissive noise and shook his head.

'No, I'm sorry. I owe you an apology. I thought—'

'That it was some dirty little affair? That we'd gone out and got drunk? Believe me, that would have been easier to deal with.'

'I'm sure. How's Jem doing?'

'Oh, he's all right, I suppose. Still sore, still got the drain and the catheter, and I don't think that pleases him, but maybe he'll have them out tomorrow.'

'Probably,' Jack agreed. 'Are they going to get him up?'

How odd, Nick thought, that Lucy could hug him and then go and cry, but Jack was here talking about his treatment, hanging onto normality.

So like him, so ready to push his emotions aside if they became inconvenient or embarrassing.

But this business with Jem was teaching him a lot about his emotions, most of it uncomfortable, and he was learning to deal with them.

Ben appeared in the doorway. 'Supper's ready when you are. There's no rush.'

'It's OK, we're ready,' Nick lied, because his guts were so knotted with tension he didn't think he could possibly eat again.

'So—what happens now?' Lucy asked, and he shrugged.

'I don't know. We're taking it a day at a time. I've found a converted barn to rent—it's near here, you probably know it. St Adwen's. It's been for sale, but they haven't managed to shift it, so they're letting it, and it's mostly single storey, with two bedrooms upstairs and two down, so when he comes out of hospital we're going to stay there for a while until he recovers. It'll give us a bit of privacy and time to be together as a family, without the pressure of having to buy anywhere.'

'What about your house?' Jack suggested. 'That's got a room downstairs he could use as a bedroom, and a shower room next to it.'

'Neither of us would feel comfortable there, under the circumstances. It's very much your mother's house, but maybe it's time I moved on.'

'Meaning?' Lucy asked, looking at him keenly.

He set his fork down, very precisely, and met her eyes.

'I'm thinking of asking Kate to give me another chance. We're going to see how it goes with Jem, but if I think we could make a go of it, I might ask her to marry me.'

Her eyes flooded again, and she got up and came and hugged him. 'Oh, Dad. I'm so pleased. I've been so worried about you on your own, and Kate's so lovely, and now we know how much you love her—'

'Hey, hey, don't jump the gun, I haven't asked her yet and she certainly hasn't said yes. It could all fall apart if Jem throws a hissy fit at the idea of us living together.'

She sat down again and propped her chin on her hand. 'Do you think he will?'

He shrugged. 'I really have no idea. He doesn't know I'm his father yet, we still have to cross that hurdle, and I have no idea how he'll react.' He sighed. 'Although with my track record maybe he'd be better off not knowing—'

His children both chipped in then, contradicting him, telling him he was a good father, the best...

'What about "My way or the highway"?' he quoted back at them from one of their recent conversations. 'What about all the morals I stuffed down your throats?'

'Well, at least you had principles, even if you weren't always strong enough to stick to them,' Jack said reasonably.

'And you've always loved us, even if you were a bit tough and uncompromising, and we've always known that,' Lucy said, reaching out and squeezing his hand. 'Don't worry. Just give him time. And we'll be there, too. Once he's better I'll take the kids in to visit. They love him, and he's their uncle, of course. I think he may find that a bit of a shock when he works it out.'

'I hadn't even thought of that,' Nick said, and picked his fork up again, suddenly hungry. 'This is good chilli, Ben. Thanks.'

'My pleasure,' Ben said, giving him a wry smile. 'There's plenty more.'

'D'you know, I don't mind if I do,' he said with a grin, and handed Ben his plate.

Kate waited for him, lying awake on the top of the bed they'd given her at the hospital, and when he called her, shortly before midnight, she told him to come up. He tapped on the door and came in and perched beside her, and she reached for his hand and held it.

'How was it?'

'Oh, pretty much as expected. They were angry at first, worried about Jem, about the impact this would have on him—you were right about them, they've taken him to their hearts, he's part of the family now whether he likes it or not. Curiously it wasn't that much about the fact that I was unfaithful to their mother, although that didn't thrill them. They seemed more concerned for him— about my provision for him in my will, about his education and what I intend to do to take care of him, and about you.'

He hesitated, then went on, 'I told them about us, about how we met, and a bit about that night— not all of it, but enough. I know you didn't want me to, but they didn't understand, and how could they, without being there, without understanding how devastated we were that night, how bonded together by our grief we were. So I tried to explain.'

'And did they understand, in the end?'

He gave a low laugh. 'I think so. I was pretty graphic. Not about us, but the rest. They apologised for making me dredge it all up—they were pretty shocked. They hadn't realised what it had been like that day, and I didn't pull any punches. I even told them about their Uncle Phil and how he died.'

'Oh, Nick,' she said, squeezing his hand tighter. 'I'm sorry you had to go through it all again.'

'It's all right. It was important that they understood, and I think they do now. I also thought they should know that Annabel sent me to make sure you were all right.'

She stared at him. 'Annabel sent you?'

'Yes. I thought you knew that?'

'How would I know, Nick? We've never talked about it—never discussed the night of the storm. I'm not sure I even know fully what happened. Will you tell me?'

'Really?'

'If you can bear to go over it all again.'

He shrugged. 'Sure. If you really want to know.'

'I do,' she said, and then, because he was still clearly running it over in his head, still chock-full of emotion, she patted the bed and shuffled over. 'Come here. You need a hug.'

For a moment he did nothing, but then with a tired sigh he lay down beside her and drew her into his arms. She put her head on his shoulder, and wrapped her arms round him and held him.

'So tell me,' she urged softly. 'Tell me how it happened.'

'Well, you know the school kids were stranded down on the rocks at the foot of the headland—that's where James was, of course, and my father was on the top of the headland, helping with the children that had been brought up the cliff while my brother was abseiling down the face and rescuing the ones still stranded. The last child's helmet had fallen off on the way up, and so Phil took his off and gave it to her, and then a huge wave—the same wave that swept James off the rocks—picked them up and threw them against the cliff and shattered his skull. My father helped pull them up, and failed to tell anyone he'd had a heart attack three weeks earlier.

'I hadn't been there at first, I was in my surgery over in Wadebridge, but I was called to help and I arrived to find my father collapsing with another heart attack, and my brother lying on the grass in the lashing rain with the back of his skull caved in. There was nothing I could do for Phil, he'd died instantly. My mother was at home, unaware of what was going on, but Annabel was in the church hall, making tea for everyone, so I told her to pick my mother up and meet us at the hospital, and I went in the ambulance with my father, trying to keep him alive when he arrested. And by the time we set off, we knew that James had been washed off the rocks by the same wave.

'I managed to keep my father going until we got to the hospital, and my mother was with him when he died, although he never recovered consciousness, and after she'd said goodbye to her husband, I had to take her down to the chapel of rest to say goodbye to her son.'

He broke off for a moment, reliving it, and beside him he heard Kate suck in a shaky breath. 'Nick, you don't have to do this.'

'It's OK,' he said softly, taking her hand and

squeezing it. 'It's time we talked about it, because otherwise it's too damned easy to say we should have known better. Anyway, I took them back to the house, Annabel and my mother, and we had tea.' He gave a shaky laugh. 'It's funny how tea always seems to come into this equation. I can't tell you how much tea and coffee I've drunk in the last couple of days. Anyway, after a while Mum started to cry—that terrible sound of grief.'

'Oh, Nick. Poor, poor woman. How on earth did she cope, losing both of them on the same day?'

'She didn't. It broke her. And on that night of course we couldn't leave her, but I couldn't stop thinking about James, and neither could Annabel. She told me to go and find you and see if there was any news of him. I think we both knew he was dead, and afterwards I wondered if she knew what she was doing when she sent me. I suspect she did. She wasn't stupid.'

It had been a bizarre conversation, most of the words unsaid, he remembered. And he could re-member, too, the look in her eyes. The under-standing, the quiet resignation. The blessing. He gave a quiet sigh and went on.

'The rest you know. I found you on the headland,

with the wind and rain lashing your clothes, and you were so cold—chilled to the bone.'

'I was waiting for you. I knew you'd come.'

'I don't know how. I just knew I had to.'

He'd undressed her and put her in the shower, and put the kettle on, just like the other day. And just like the other day, he'd heard her crying, like his mother, with inconsolable grief, and he'd gone to her. The woman he loved, the girl he'd fallen for. The woman, he realised, he still loved with all his heart. He closed his eyes and swallowed.

He paused, remembering that he'd already stripped off his saturated, blood-stained shirt, and he'd taken off the rest and gone into the shower and put his arms around her and held her, and she'd clung to him, just as she'd clung to him that morning, and they'd cried together. He had no idea how long for. Ten minutes? An hour?

He wasn't really sure what had happened then. He hadn't understood it at the time and he still didn't understand it now, but they'd needed each other in a way so deep, so elemental that there had been no denying it. They were both angry, furious that something so crazy had happened to kill two young, healthy men with years ahead of them and an old man who should have lived to

enjoy his retirement and instead had been snuffed
out like a candle.

Maybe it was just defiance, and the fact that
people they'd loved had died so senselessly, and it
was almost as if they'd had to prove to themselves
that they were still alive, but there had been no
stopping it, no reasoning, just a soul-deep need
that had driven them half-crazed into each other's
arms.

Afterwards he'd turned off the water and dried
her and put her to bed and then he'd gone home
and showered and changed and gone back to his
wife. They'd never spoken of it again, but after
that, nothing had been quite the same...

'Nick?'

He started a little and stared at Kate, then shook
his head to clear it of the unwanted, haunting
images.

'I'm sorry that night was so awful for you all,'
she whispered. 'Thank you for telling me. And
I'm sorry the kids were hard on you.'

'It's OK. It's over now, and I'm glad it's out in
the open. I think they realise now that it wasn't
a premeditated decision to betray their mother,
or that Jem was conceived as a drunken result of
some sordid little date, just two people, who had

always cared about each other, on the edge of despair and reaching out to each other that night.'

'We weren't ourselves. No wonder we didn't think about contraception, not then and not afterwards.'

'I did, but not till weeks later, when you told me you were pregnant, and I asked you if it was my child, and you said no. And I accepted it without question, with relief, even, because I didn't ever want to have to think of that night again. But you knew, didn't you? You knew he was mine because of the fertility problems.'

'Yes. Yes, I knew. James's notes had gone back to the PCT when he died, so I'd had to ring the clinic and ask them for the results, and they'd told me that James was sterile. But I couldn't tell you. Not then. It wouldn't have achieved anything and so many more people would have been hurt. But maybe now we can move on.'

'Maybe.'

He turned his head, and she lifted her face and their lips met in a gentle, tender kiss that made her heart skip a beat. He shifted, turning towards her, and their legs tangled, their bodies hard against each other.

'Nick, we can't,' she whispered, and he sighed, his breath soft against her cheek.

'I know. I just need to hold you.'

But he kept on kissing her, his lips tracing soft circles over her cheeks, her eyes, her throat.

'Nick…'

'Shh. It's all right,' he murmured, drawing her closer again and settling her head on his shoulder once more. 'I'm going in a minute.'

Except he didn't. He was asleep in seconds, emotionally exhausted, and although her arm had gone to sleep, she didn't have the heart to wake him. So she lay there for an hour, until he stirred and gave a sleepy grunt, and she murmured his name.

'Sorry—I didn't mean to doze off. Are you all right?' he asked, sitting up and shifting out of her way.

'I'm fine. My arm's dead, though.'

He tutted and took it in his hands, rubbing it briskly until the pins and needles had gone and she sighed with relief, and then he stood up. 'I ought to go home. How's Jem been? Did he go to sleep all right?'

'Yes, he's fine. And Sam and Gemma have a

baby boy. They're calling him Archie—Archie Nicholas, for you.'

She heard him suck in his breath, and then let it out again, obviously touched by the gesture. 'That's great. How are they?'

'Well. Fine. The baby's beautiful, and Gemma's OK, it was a nice, straightforward delivery. It was lovely to see them. A bit of normality, really. They send their love.'

'I'll pop up tomorrow, take them something. And I ought to bring Jem in something, but I have no idea what. I don't want to look as if I'm trying to buy him,' he said with a wry grin, and she laughed.

'So bring him grapes. He adores grapes, and he needs fruit on all these opiates.'

'Grapes? Lucy gives him a games console that probably cost well over a hundred pounds, and you suggest I bring him grapes?' he said, laughing softly.

'Or you could look as if you're trying to buy him,' she said reasonably, and he sighed.

'OK. Grapes it is. And I suppose the games console's only on loan.'

It was, although of course he could always buy him his own, she thought, but she didn't suggest it. Time enough later for extravagant gestures, and she'd rather he didn't get into the habit of playing on a games machine as a regular thing.

He bent and kissed her cheek, then lifted his head slightly, stared into her eyes and slowly lowered his head again, touching his lips to hers once more. Just briefly, very lightly, but it was like being stroked with fire.

'Sleep tight. I'll see you in the morning,' he murmured, and he went out and closed the door softly behind him, leaving her lying there with her fingers on her lips, and her body tingling with anticipation.

CHAPTER SEVEN

NICK didn't arrive until ten the next day, to her surprise.

By the time he came in, Martin Bradley had been round, and as Jem seemed comfortable, the surgeon said he could try sitting up a little in bed, instead of just having his head and shoulders being propped up.

It ached a bit, Jem said, but Kate could tell he was happier. He was getting so bored lying down, and sitting up properly he was able to play with the games console to his heart's content while she sat beside him with a magazine and let it all go on around her.

Her presence was less essential now than it had been. He was no longer in danger, and he was used to the staff, familiar with his surroundings and happier about being left.

She'd already decided the night before that it would be the last time she stayed, and she was getting desperate for her own bed.

Or at least one that didn't have a plastic mattress.

If Nick would only arrive, she thought, she could talk to him about the barn. She hadn't told Jem yet what their plans were, she wanted to do that with Nick, preferably before he signed on the dotted line at the letting agent's, but when he arrived he dangled a bunch of keys in front of her with a smug grin, like a magician pulling a rabbit out of a hat.

'Your keys, ma'am,' he said, dropping them into her hand. 'You can move in whenever you like.'

She was at the nurses' station, out in the ward, talking to the ward sister and Megan Phillips about what was to happen next, and she stared at the keys in slight consternation.

'What's the matter?' he said, his voice dropping. 'I thought that was what you wanted?'

'It is,' she said. 'But—I thought we were going to talk to Jem first? What if he says no?'

'What if he does? He's ten years old, Kate. There are some decisions that aren't his to make. This is a temporary fix, for a few weeks initially, to cover his convalescence. His friends can come and visit, he can treat it as a holiday—and if it doesn't work out, if he doesn't want me around, then I can go home. It doesn't change anything. It's just for now.'

He was right, of course—he was always right, she thought, except when he was wrong, and then it tended to be on an epic scale. But this—this was just common sense, and she let her breath out on a little huff of laughter and tried to smile.

'You're right. I'm sorry, it's not as if it's a permanent thing. I'm being silly.'

And she'd been letting herself get carried away with all the possibilities. A temporary fix, she reminded herself. Just that, nothing more, for a few weeks, and it might be a total disaster on several counts.

'This might be more long term,' he said then, pulling another set of keys from his pocket, and dropping them in her hand too.

She glanced down, and blinked. 'Car keys?'

'Mmm. I wasn't sure what you wanted, so I asked Chloe if you'd said anything. She mentioned a model you liked.'

She stared at the keys, confused. 'You've got me a car on the PCT contract this quickly?' she said. Surely she had to sign something...

'No. I've bought you a Golf—a nice economical

little diesel. They're delivering it to the barn this afternoon.'

She stared at him as if he'd gone mad. 'You bought me a new car?'

'No. It's not new. It's two years old. I thought you'd shout at me if I got you a new one.'

She opened her mouth to shout at him anyway, and to her horror a little sob came out instead.

'Kate?'

'Sorry,' she said, flapping her hand and blinking hard. 'I— It's just— Oh, Nick, you didn't have to do that. I could have got myself another car. Renting the house is one thing, this is quite another. You're doing too much, going too fast.'

'No, I'm not.' This one's got a much better NCAP crash rating. I'm not trying to bribe you,' he said grimly, 'I'm trying—too late—to make sure my son stays safe.'

She swallowed, unable to argue, filled with guilt that her car had contributed to his injuries, but he misunderstood her silence and sighed.

'I'm sorry. I know I interfere. It doesn't matter, you can use it for the moment and once you get yourself the car you want, I'll give it to Lucy or something, make it a pool car for the practice maybe.'

'No!' She closed her hand around the keys, reached up and kissed his cheek. 'Thank you. I was just stunned, that's all. I've had to rely on myself for so long, and— Oh, damn.'

Her eyes were welling up, and she rummaged for a tissue in her pocket. He got there first, plucking one off the top of the nurses' station and handing it to her, and she blew her nose and sniffed hard. 'Sorry. It's been a bit of a roller-coaster.'

'I know. How is he?'

She filled him in on the day's events, and he went in to see Jem while she packed her things in the little room she'd been using and gave herself a thorough talking to. She handed the key back to the staff nurse and thanked her, and went into Jem's room to find Nick perched beside him on the bed, leaning up against the backrest and watching him with the games console while he ate grapes.

'You could put that down for five minutes, you know,' she pointed out, but Jem just grinned.

'Uncle Nick wanted to see how I was doing. I was just showing him. I've been teaching him how to use it.'

She stared at him, realising how easily these two had slipped into an easy relationship, almost as if Jem knew Nick was his father. He must have been so desperate for a father all these years, she thought, and he'd never said a word about it; perhaps he didn't realise it, even now. She'd thought he was all right, that they were fine on their own, but maybe she'd been deluding herself and all the time there'd been a void.

A void that should have been filled by Nick.

'We've got something to talk to you about,' she said, determined to get the barn out into the open. 'Could you put that down and listen, please?'

He looked up at her, his eyes wary, and then looked down again. 'Oh, no, it killed me!' he wailed, and put the console down on the locker, then looked up at her again a little worriedly. 'What did you want to talk about?'

'You. When you come out of here, you might not be able to walk up and down stairs for a while, and we've got no bathroom downstairs.'

'Oh. Does that mean I'll have to stay in here longer, till I can go upstairs?' he asked miserably. 'I don't want to. I want to go home as soon as I can. It's not the same here.'

'I know. And, no, it doesn't mean that. It means we'll have to stay somewhere else for a little while. Uncle N—' She broke off, met Nick's eyes

ruefully and went on, 'Uncle Nick's found somewhere for us, somewhere he can stay, too, just
outside Penhally, near Ben and Lucy. It's a barn,
and it's got a downstairs bedroom with doors out
to the garden, and an en suite wetroom—'

'What's a non-sweet wetroom?'

'En suite—it's French. It means it's a bathroom
attached just to one bedroom. And a wetroom
means it's got a tiled floor and you just walk into
it and shower, so you wouldn't even have to step
up to a shower tray.'

'Wow. And we can stay there?'

'Yes.'

'And you're coming?' he asked, swivelling his
head round to look at Nick, and he nodded.

'Yes—so I can help out, and I can do stuff for
you that you might not want your mum doing,
like help you shower and so on, if you need help
at first.'

He nodded. 'Can the dog come?'

'Yes.'

'OK. So was that all you want to talk about?'

She met Nick's eyes and they were full of relief
and wry humour. She smiled. 'Nothing else. Just
that.'

'Oh. Well, can I try and get to the next level, then? I was nearly there and then it killed me.'

'Kids.'
'Don't. I can't believe he took it so well.'
'Of course he did,' Nick said as if it was obvious, and put the tray down on the table. 'He trusts you to take care of him. You've done it—made it possible for him to be discharged as soon as it's practicable. Why should he take it any other way?'

'Because we always talk everything through. Before I do anything, we talk it through. We're not impulsive like you.'

He looked at her as if she had two heads, and she thought of Lucy and Jack pointing out to him that he interfered, and stifled a smile.

'Don't laugh at me. I'm not impulsive, I'm decisive. It's different,' he protested.

'Actually, you're both,' she pointed out gently, reaching for her coffee. 'Nick, you're going to have to get used to him. Jem likes to see all sides of a thing before he'll commit to it. If I say jump, he doesn't ask how high, he asks why. And I know it's an alien concept to you, but it's the way I've brought him up.'

'It's not an alien concept,' he disagreed, stirring his coffee with huge concentration. 'It's just that some things are as they are. He has to know that there isn't always an answer, that sometimes you have to take some things and some people on trust.'

'And you know what he'd say to that?'

'"Why?"' they said together, and then laughed, reaching out and linking their fingers on the table.

'Did you get anything for Gemma's baby?' she asked, and he nodded.

'Yes. I found a lovely pop-up book of farm animals. It's not for now, obviously, but I thought he might like it later.'

'That's a lovely idea, and it goes really well with my present. I've knitted him a little jumper with fluffy sheep on the front.'

He frowned quizzically. 'Really? You can knit?'

She laughed. 'Of course I can knit! All women can knit.'

'Annabel couldn't knit.'

She felt her smile die. 'Nick, I'm not Annabel,' she reminded him gently. 'And that's not a criticism of her, it's just a fact.'

He closed his eyes for a second and sighed. 'I know you're not Annabel. I'm only too aware of who you are. I just didn't know you could knit. It's one of the very many things I don't know about you, that I've never had the chance to find out. I didn't mean to offend you by comparing you to Annabel.'

'I'm not offended,' she said quickly. 'Not at all. But we are—were—different. You need to realise that if we're going to live together.'

'Well, then, isn't it a good job that I've already noticed?' he said softly, and, draining his coffee, he got to his feet. 'There's Lucy—she said she'd try and pop in. Come on, we'll go up with her.'

He held out his hand to help Kate up, and then tucked her hand in the crook of his arm. 'Hello, darling,' he said, kissing his daughter's cheek, and she took his other arm and walked with them to the ward.

'I've got something for you, from Ben. His chilli recipe. He says you can look after Kate, spoil her a little. Here.'

He grinned and tucked it in his pocket, and vowed to make it for her soon.

They left Jem with Lucy, telling him they were going to see the barn and would be back later, and twenty minutes later they'd pulled up outside and unlocked the door.

'Welcome home,' he said softly, pushing the door open, and she stepped inside, a little bit of her disappointed that he hadn't carried her over the threshold. But how stupid was that? They weren't married—far from it, and they might never be. This was just about Jem, and if she'd expected more because of his tenderness with her last night, she was deluded.

The entrance was in the single-story section on the left-hand side, between the living space and the bedrooms, and they walked through to the sitting room with its low beamed ceiling and comfortable furniture grouped around the log burner, and into the central section where a battered old oak refectory table sat in pride of place.

It would be the perfect setting for family get-togethers, she thought—all Nick's children with their spouses and families gathered around, the air filled with their laughter. She could hear it now, as she looked around her at the great vaulted space of the dining hall. Its huge, soaring window faced the courtyard, with its flat, winding paths and low shrubs giving structure to the sheltered little garden, the wings of the house wrapped round it like arms, protecting it from the elements, and then beyond it were the fields and then the sea.

And like Nick had the first time he'd stepped inside, she felt the house welcome her, as if those arms had folded round her and gathered her to its heart.

Romantic nonsense, she thought, and yet…

'You were right, it is calm and tranquil here,' she said softly, feeling the tension drain out of her. 'It'll be so good for him. Thank you, Nick.'

And going up on tiptoe, she kissed his cheek.

For a long moment he stared at her, their eyes locked, and then he seemed to pull himself together and looked away, and they walked around the rest of the house slowly and had their first real, proper look.

'It's amazing,' she said, standing on the galleried walkway above the dining hall and looking out over the courtyard to the sea in the distance. 'Beautiful. I could stand here all day and look at that view.'

'There are plenty of chairs you could sit on,' Nick pointed out with a smile, and she laughed softly and turned away from the window, looking up at the vaulted ceiling with its heavy beams.

The gallery spanned the space, leading to a bed-room at each end, and they were both amazing.

'Which bedroom do you want?'

She glanced at him. 'I don't know. Maybe I should be downstairs with Jem. He could call me then, if he needed me in the night.'

And she'd be further from temptation.

'It doesn't have its own shower.'

'There's a bathroom almost next to it. I'm sure I'll manage.' She went back downstairs and round the corner to the wing with the two bedrooms and the study in it, on the other side of the en-trance hall. The bedroom there which she would take was a small room in comparison to the ones upstairs, but big enough for her, and most impor-tantly it was close to Jem's.

'It'll be fine,' she said firmly, and he nodded. She wasn't sure, but she thought he looked a tiny bit relieved. 'What about you?'

He gave a wry smile. 'If there's no competi-tion, I'll have the one with the sea view from the window by the bed.'

It also had a view of her bedroom window, she realised, glancing out of it and looking up at the taller section of the barn. 'We ought to get some food in,' she said, trying to be practical and not think about his bedroom.

'I've done it. I ordered it on line last night. It's being delivered in the morning between seven and nine.'

'Will you be here?'

'Yes. I thought I'd stay here tonight, start moving some things in. I ought to go into the practice tomorrow, too, and catch up on some admin. I can't just bail on them, and Jem seems to be improving steadily. I'll take you over there whenever you like so you can be with him, if you don't feel ready to drive yet. Just tell me when you want to be picked up.'

'After the shopping arrives?'

He nodded. 'Sure. I'll come and get you from your place once it's here.'

'Or I could stay here, too,' she said rashly, and his eyes locked with hers.

'You could.'

But their eyes remained locked, both of them trapped, like rabbits in headlights, transfixed by the prospect of being alone together in this house.

Nick dragged his eyes away. 'Of course you could move in, start getting settled, and I could stay at home. And you could get the dog back from Chloe and Oliver. He must miss you.'

'But I can't really leave him alone here, he's not used to it. He'd be better in our puppy crèche until Jem's out of hospital, at least for the days. And I'm not sure how safe the garden is. I don't want him getting out.'

'There's a fenced area—I had a look at it this morning on my way to the agents. I couldn't get into the house, but I walked all round the garden, and the back of it's entirely enclosed to about four feet in height with sheep netting. He'd be quite safe. He could just run around and let off steam when you're here, and he could go to the puppy crèche when neither of us is around. And I can come over and help you walk him.'

'But you've ordered food. It should be you here, not me.'

'I can eat with you. You have to eat, too, Kate. As Ben said, I can wait on you,' he said with a wry smile, and she chuckled.

'I can just see that.'

'Let me try. You never know, I might be good at it. One of my hidden talents.'

She gave a splutter of laughter. 'Very successfully hidden. You've kept it from me for thirty-four years,' she said drily, and went back to the kitchen to acquaint herself with it.

She heard a quiet sigh behind her, and turned back to him, shocked by the sadness in his eyes. 'Oh, Nick...'

'I'm sorry,' he said, his voice bleak. 'It wasn't the way it was meant to be, was it?'

'What?'

'Life. Our plans.'

'We don't always get what we're expecting in life,' she said gently. 'I always thought you'd come back from university and marry me and I'd have your children. Instead you married Annabel, and I married James, and we couldn't have any, and you ended up with loads.'

'Was that why you gave up midwifery? Because it hurt too much not being able to have your own?'

She smiled. 'That and watching you and Annabel bring the children down here on holiday year after year when they were little. All the children I might have had if I'd been with you, and yet there I was with James, banging our heads against a brick wall. And then you moved back down here close to your family and got a job in Wadebridge and bought the house on Harbour

Road, and I was falling over you all the time, a constant reminder of what I'd lost.'

He sighed heavily. 'Kate, don't. We can't turn the clock back.'

'No. But even if we haven't gone home together every night, I've worked with you for years now in the practice. I've seen you every day, spent time with you, so it hasn't all been bad,' she pointed out gently. 'You've still been part of my life. And I have Jem. You can have no idea what that's meant to me, over the years.'

'I can imagine. My children are infinitely precious to me, even though I haven't always seen eye to eye with them, so you don't have to try and explain.'

She smiled sadly, wishing that Jem had been one of those precious children, that she'd been their mother, but, as he said, they couldn't turn the clock back and if they did, it would all be very different. And so she couldn't wish it undone, no matter how hard it had been at times.

He came over to her, standing just inches away, and with the tip of a long forefinger he tilted her head up so she met his eyes. 'Don't be sad, Kate. We've got a chance now, if we choose to take it. Let's not waste it.'

A chance? For them? So maybe she hadn't misunderstood. 'I still don't know how good you could be at waiting on me,' she said lightly, and he laughed.

'Oh, I'm good,' he said, his eyes twinkling with mischief, and she sucked in a tiny little breath and turned away, before she did something silly, like kiss him. He'd kissed her last night, but that had been in the safety of the hospital, where anyone could have come in. They were alone here, and awareness of that and of him made her tingle with nerves.

'I'm looking forward to finding out,' she said lightly. 'So, are you moving in here tonight, or am I?'

'Do you want to?'

'Not alone. It makes me feel a bit nervous,' she admitted. She held her breath for a second, then said, 'We could always be grown up about it and share.'

His mouth twisted into something that could have been a smile if it hadn't been so touched with sadness.

'Grown-ups sleep together, Kate,' he said softly. 'And I'm not sure you're ready for that yet.'

Her heart hammered against her ribcage. 'Can't we have a little restraint?'

'Oh, yes. We can have a little. I just think it might take rather more than that.'

She looked away, his eyes too revealing suddenly, full of feelings that had been locked away for very many years. Her tongue flicked out and moistened her lips, and he groaned.

'Kate, don't,' he whispered, his voice almost inaudible.

The air was vibrating with tension, almost solid, as if she could cut it with a knife, and it seemed to have set all around them, holding them in place, their eyes locked again.

The sound of the doorbell was shocking, dissolving the air so they could move again, and Nick walked to the door as if he was in a trance.

He opened it and looked past the man standing on the broad flagstone path. There were three cars outside. His, and two others.

Of course. Kate's new car.

'Delivery for Mrs Althorp?' the man said, brandishing a clipboard and some keys, and he gave himself a mental shake and breathed in.

'Yes—thank you. Kate?'

'I'm here,' she said, coming to stand beside him. 'Is that it?'

'The metallic grey one,' he said, his voice sounding strained. 'You have to sign for it.'

'You'd better check it over,' the man said.

It could have had square wheels, for all the attention they gave it. Kate could see nothing but the look in Nick's eyes, he could see nothing but her tongue flicking out to lick her lips.

'It's fine,' he said, and she signed the sheet with trembling fingers and the delivery driver handed her the keys.

'Enjoy your car, then,' he said, and drove away in the other vehicle, leaving them standing there.

'So, will it be all right? The car?' he asked, trying desperately for normality, and she nodded.

Not that she was really able to concentrate on it, but it was exactly what she'd wanted, top of her wish list, and she was thrilled with it. She would be thrilled with it, just the moment she could get that look in his eyes out of her head.

'It's wonderful. Thank you, Nick. I'll look after it, I promise.'

'No. I'll look after it. I've bought a service

package with it. It's got the next three years of servicing paid for. All you have to do is book it in.'

Her eyes filled. He seemed to have thought of everything, and she ought to pay a bit more attention to it after all his trouble and expense. She sat in the driver's seat, and rested her head back with a sigh.

'All right?'

'Lovely. Really good seat. Gosh, it's nice to rest my head. My neck's still a bit achy.'

He gave a short sigh and held the door for her. 'Come on, you need to lie down, and I'm going to massage it for you,' he said firmly, and, locking the car, he ushered her back inside and down the corridor to her bedroom.

'We'll need to bring bed linen,' she said, clutching at normality.

'Yes. What have you got on under that top?' he asked, and she swallowed.

'A vest top and a bra.'

'Right. Take the top off, leave the vest top on and lie down on your back with your head at the foot of the bed,' he instructed in a businesslike doctor's voice, and then he covered her with her top so only her shoulders were exposed, put a pillow under her knees, knelt down on the floor by her head and slid his warm, hard hands under her shoulders, running his fingers gently but firmly up the columns of muscle each side of her spine and up into her neck.

'Oh, that's amazing,' she groaned, and he said nothing, just kept on with the gentle, rhythmic movement until the tension had eased out of her neck and shoulders and she was utterly relaxed. Then he got to his feet and stood looking down at her, an odd expression in his eyes.

'Stay there for a while, have a rest. I won't be long.'

'What are you going to do?'

'Get us some milk from the Trevellyans' farm shop, and something for supper. I'll only be a few minutes, it's just up the road. Try and have a sleep.'

She heard the front door close behind him, and then the sound of a car driving away, crunching on the gravel. Odd, how they hadn't heard the other two arrive, but, then, she'd not been able to hear anything over the pounding of her heart.

She got up and pulled her top back on, lay down the right way up with a pillow under her head, and curled on her side, staring unseeingly out of the French doors at the courtyard beyond.

There. They'd managed it—been in a bedroom, had their hands on each other, even, and survived it.

They could do this. Behave like grown-ups.

Grown-ups sleep together, Kate.

'Not if they choose not to,' she said out loud, and closed her eyes determinedly. Before she knew it, she'd drifted off to sleep.

He wasn't long—just long enough to give himself some much-needed sea air and take Kate's new car out for a spin. He drove to the Trevellyans' with the windows open and the wind in his hair, and by the time he'd returned with the shopping, he was almost back under control.

He pottered round the kitchen, putting everything away while the kettle boiled and investigating the contents of the cupboards. It was such a blessing that the place was furnished as a holiday cottage and equipped with everything. It meant they only had to bring clothes and bedding, and they could pick them up later. Or whoever was staying would. He still wasn't sure who it would be.

The kettle boiled, and he made a pot of tea, left it to brew and tapped on her door.

There was no reply, and when he opened the door he saw she was fast asleep on her side, her hand lying open, relaxed, the fingers loosely curled. He stood there for a few moments, watching the slow rise and fall of her chest, and as if she'd become aware of him she opened her eyes and looked up.

'Oh. You're back,' she said softly.

'I've made tea. It's in the kitchen. And Mike Trevellyan sends his love.'

'Oh, you saw him.'

'Yes. And he'd heard a rumour about me and Jem. I told him it was true. He won't spread it further, but I thought he ought to know. And, anyway, they're Ben and Lucy's neighbours.'

'Yes, of course. So it's out, is it?'

She sat up on the edge of the bed and ran her hands through her hair, lifting it away from her neck and letting it fall, and he felt heat slam through him.

'It seems that way.' He walked away, heading back to the kitchen before he did something he'd regret. 'I've poured the tea,' he called over his shoulder, 'and I bought one of Fran's lemon drizzle cakes.'

She followed him, tugging her top straight and reminding him of what was underneath it. Not that he needed reminding, after kneeling by her head and staring down her cleavage for ten minutes. 'That's my favourite,' she said with a smile.

'I know. That's why I bought it.'

He slid a plate towards her with a generous slice on it, and followed it with a cup of tea, and she sat down at the table overlooking the courtyard and the sea and smiled again.

'I could learn to love it here,' she said.

He sat down beside her, propped his elbows on the table and looked out at the view while he bit into the cake.

'Good. Me, too. So, who's moving in when?'

'Both of us. Tonight,' she said firmly, and he nearly choked. He couldn't blow it, he reminded himself. It was too important, there was far too much at stake.

He could do this. He could.

Even if it killed him.

CHAPTER EIGHT

WATCHING Jem slowly recover his strength was both a joy and a relief, but unbelievably draining.

Every hour brought further progress—sitting up in bed, then sitting out, then standing for a moment on his right leg as he swivelled onto the chair for himself. It was like watching a time-lapse sequence of a baby turning into a toddler, but Kate was more than happy to sit through it. She was looking forward to seeing him walk again, to seeing him run, but for now, she was just glad he was alive and making progress.

And to know she'd be going home to the barn every night with Nick. She felt that if she pinched herself, she'd wake up and find it was all a dream, and the thought was frightening.

They'd moved in last night, collecting just enough clothes and linen to see them over the next few days, and then he'd cooked for her—not Ben's chilli, but a cold chicken and ham pie from the farm shop, with a lovely fresh salad and boiled new potatoes, followed by some utterly delectable honey and ginger ice cream made on the farm.

And they'd talked about telling Jem. Today. Later, after Nick arrived. He was at the surgery now, doing a clinic and seeing a few patients, and then he was coming over and they were going to tell him.

Somehow. She still had no idea how.

She went for a walk up the corridor to see Gemma and her baby while they took out Jem's catheter, to his relief, and then they moved him to the ward downstairs, which was for the children who were on the mend; it had access on one side to a courtyard with seats and toys and lots of things to look at, and on the other side, right near his bed, was the courtyard with the ducklings.

Five of them, they finally concluded, watching them peck about amongst the moss and bark chips, brown and yellow and fluffy and very cute. They watched them for ages, until at last the mother tucked them back under her wings for a rest, and he went back to his games console.

He was allowed other visitors now, and the first people to come in the afternoon were Rob and Matthew.

The boys had plenty to talk about and they left them to it. Rob took her hand and squeezed it fleetingly. 'How are you? It must have been hell—have you coped OK?'

She nodded. 'Yes. It's been pretty awful, but Nick's been great. Rob—there's something you need to know.'

He shook his head and smiled. 'I know already—I can see it in your eyes, and I'm really pleased for you. You go for it. I know how you feel. Your heart will never really belong to anybody else, just as mine won't, but at least you've now got that chance, and you have to take it.' He glanced at Jem, his head close to Matt's, bent over the games console. 'Does Jem know yet?' he asked softly.

'The paternity thing?' she murmured. 'No. Or about Nick and me. That's so new I'm not sure I know about it, really.'

He smiled. 'I think Jem will be fine with it once he's used to the idea. Is there anything I can do, anything I can get you?'

She shook her head. 'No. Just bring Matt to see him sometimes. He's going to be horribly bored. Oh, and we've taken a rented barn up near the Trevellyans' farm, with some bedrooms and a shower room on the ground floor, in case he can't manage stairs for a while. I'll give you the directions. Matt can come and stay later on, if you like. It'll give Jem something to look forward to when he comes out.'

'That would be really nice. Look, is Nick all right about this? He does realise I'm just bringing Matt to see Jem?'

'Yes, he does. And he's fine with it. He likes you.'

Rob laughed softly. 'That's good of him. I'm not sure I'd be so generous in his shoes. I hope you can make this work.'

So did she, but they still had the hurdle of the great reveal, as she was beginning to call it in her head, and she couldn't really think past that.

They didn't stay long, and Nick appeared soon afterwards. She wondered if he'd been lurking somewhere, waiting until the coast was clear, giving them space.

She didn't know. He'd been a little odd with her that morning, maybe because of the barn and being there alone together. She'd gone to bed early, closing her door quite firmly, and he'd gone up a short while later. She'd seen his light come on, seen it go off shortly afterwards, and she wondered if he'd slept as well as her. They were both tired, both drained, and he'd looked better at breakfast, but he'd been quiet, a little distracted.

'So, how's it going?' he asked Jem. 'Worked your way up another level yet?'

'My battery's flat again,' he said. 'I had to ask the nurses upstairs to charge it, but I don't know any of the nurses down here so I don't know who to ask.'

'I can charge it for you,' he said. 'We've got to go soon—we're going to pick Bruno up from Chloe and take him back to the barn and settle him in, so it can be charging while we do that and we can bring it back this evening.'

'Great—and then can we do the face thing on it, Uncle Nick?'

'Yes, I'm sure we can,' he said, and there was a flicker of emotion in his eyes, just as there always was when Jem called him that. And Kate got a stupid lump in her throat, just as she always did. But maybe not for much longer. She felt a shiver of dread, and stifled it. It would be fine. It would.

He found the charger in the locker, and packed

it up with the console and put it in her bag, and they went back to the barn, put it on charge and collected Bruno. He was so excited to see her, she thought the young dog was going to wag his tail right off, and her eyes filled with tears.

'Oh, sweetheart, have you missed me? I'm so sorry,' she said, getting down on the floor with him and hugging him, but he was too excited, and bounced around barking, and Chloe laughed and let him out into the garden so he could race round like a lunatic and have a mad five minutes with Chloe and Oliver's little bitch from the same litter of flat-coated retriever puppies.

'It's been a bit hectic on the puppy-sitting front this last week,' Chloe admitted when Kate thanked her yet again for her kindness. 'I haven't even had time to see Gemma yet—how's the baby?'

Kate smiled. 'Gorgeous. He's absolutely gorgeous. I had the nicest cuddle yesterday morning. One of the advantages of being a midwife—I can pull rank and sneak in outside visiting hours! But they were coming home today, so you should be able to pop over there anytime over the weekend.'

'Oh, I will, don't worry!' Chloe laughed. 'I'll

give her ten minutes to settle in, and I'll be there. Right, young man, back inside and settle down, and then I think you're going to go to your new home. That'll be a bit exciting, won't it?'

Bruno wagged and leant up against her leg, tongue lolling and a big smile on his face, and Kate clipped his lead on.

'Come on, you big hussy. That's enough flirting,' Nick said, and put him in his crate in the back of his estate car—much, much easier to transport him in—and they drove back to the barn and introduced him to the house.

'It's a good job they don't mind pets here,' she said, wondering how much damage he would do, but he hadn't wrecked anything at home yet, and she hoped if he settled here quickly, there wouldn't be a problem.

'Can you put him in the crate, if necessary?' Nick asked, reading her mind, and she nodded.

'Yes, but I hardly ever use it, he's been so good. And I've got him a new rope toy to play with. That might keep him occupied.'

They took him out and let him run around in the garden, and he christened a few of the bushes and came back inside, flopping down in a patch of sunshine on the wooden floor of the dining room and watching them from under his eyebrows as they made a pot of tea.

'We mustn't forget to take this back,' Kate said, checking the charge on the games console while Nick poured the tea, and while she waited for it to cool and stared at the view, he cut them thick slices of the lemon drizzle cake and put one down in front of her.

'I'll be like a house,' she protested, but he just smiled.

'You haven't put an ounce on in years,' he told her. 'You work too hard.'

'Well, I'm not working now.'

'No, but you haven't been eating in the hospital.'

'That's rubbish, I've been eating junk food! Except for the pie last night, and that was hardly low calorie.'

'It was good, though, and let's face it, a little weight on you won't hurt. You'll just get curvier, and there's nothing wrong with that. You've got a beautiful body, Kate. Be proud of it.'

She met his eyes and saw the heat flicker in them before he banked it, and she felt tears clog her throat. He didn't know what he was talking about. Maybe once, but not any more. Not since her surgery.

She looked away. 'I'd rather not gain if I can avoid it,' she said, 'so I hope you're planning something low calorie for supper.'

'Not tonight,' he said with a wry laugh. 'Tonight is Ben's chilli, but I'll cut down on the oil and it's extra-lean steak mince. And kidney beans are good for you. Anyway, you'll love it, it's a great recipe—assuming I can pull it off.'

She raised an eyebrow. 'Isn't it a bit ambitious for you?' she asked, glad to get off the topic of her body. 'I mean, I know you're trying to spoil me, but we all know you're the king of the ready meals aisle.'

He laughed and picked up his cake. 'I don't know. We'll see, won't we?' He took a bite of the cake and put it down, then stared back out of the window, his smile fading. A quiet sigh eased from his body, and he turned to her, his eyes troubled.

'How are we going to tell him, Kate?' he asked softly.

She gave a helpless little shrug. 'I have absolutely no idea.'

* * *

In the end, it was easy.

Jem was sitting up in his bed when they arrived, waiting for them. They gave him the games console and settled themselves down, Kate on the armchair by the bed where he sat during the day when he was allowed out, and Nick on a hard plastic chair facing them, so they could both see him.

There was a child in a bed near Jem who was having a blood transfusion, and he looked around, his eyes tracking to his drip and up to the bag of blood running slowly into him. He watched it drip for a moment, then said thoughtfully, 'I wonder who my blood came from?'

She saw Nick stiffen slightly, and their eyes met. Was this it? The time? She felt her heart thump against her ribs, and he gave her an imperceptible nod.

'It could have been Uncle Nick,' she said quietly. 'Or Jack. They took some from both of them. You're B-negative—it's a fairly rare blood group and they'd run out, and you have to have the same otherwise it makes you very ill.'

'And you're the same as me?' he asked, looking straight at Nick.

She saw his jaw clench. 'Yes.'

'That was lucky. Are you the same, Mum?'

She shook her head. 'No.' His head swivelled back to Nick. 'So how did they know we were the same?'

'They tested you. I know mine, because I give blood regularly. So does Jack.' He hesitated, then said carefully, 'You inherit the genes that determine your blood group from one or other of your parents,' he said, and then waited.

Jem frowned. 'So—my dad must have been B-negative, too, then?'

'Yes.'

It wasn't strictly true. His father could have been AB, but they both knew he wasn't, and thankfully Nick didn't complicate it any more than it already was. Because the essence of it was already registering, Kate could see.

'And it's rare?' Jem was saying, a little frown pleating his brow, and she saw the muscle in Nick's jaw flicker again.

'Yes. Yes, it's rare. Less than three in a hundred people.'

The frown deepened, and his eyes swivelled to Kate's. 'That's weird.'

'Not really.' She could feel her heart pounding, and she swallowed before continuing, 'Jem, there's something you need to know, something I should have told you before.'

She saw the light dawn in his eyes, and he turned his head slowly back to Nick and stared at him hard. 'Are you my father?' he asked, his voice flat.

She saw Nick's throat work, and he nodded slightly. 'Yes,' he said, his voice gruff. 'Yes, I am.'

For an endless moment he just stared at Nick in silence, and Kate could see the pulse beating in his throat.

'But—how? I thought— Why didn't you tell me? Why did you tell me my dad was dead?' he asked, turning back to Kate and spearing her with accusing eyes. 'I thought I didn't have a father, but if Uncle Nick's my father, I could have had a dad all my life! Why didn't you tell me?'

Her stomach knotted into a ball at the look in his eyes. 'I couldn't. Nick was married, he had a family, and I didn't think making them all sad would make us any happier, and it wouldn't have helped us. We had each other, Jem. We were all right—'

'No, we weren't! I didn't have a dad. I wanted a dad—I've always wanted a dad. But I thought he was dead, and all the time he was alive and you didn't tell me! If I hadn't had the accident, if I hadn't needed his blood, would you have told me? Ever?'

She swallowed down the tears. 'Of course I would. I always knew I'd have to tell you one day when the time was right, I just didn't know when that would be. We've been trying to work out how to do it without hurting you.'

He stared reproachfully at her, then at Nick again, and asked him a question she'd asked herself over and over. 'Why don't you want to be my dad?'

Nick flinched as if he'd been kicked in the gut. 'I do.'

'You don't,' Jem said firmly. 'When we were on the beach flying the kite, ages ago, after Christmas last year, that American lady said I was like my father, and I laughed, and you said you couldn't do this and stormed off. I didn't understand, but that was it, wasn't it? She realised you were my dad, and you didn't want me to know, so you walked away, because you don't want to be my father.'

'I do.'

'No, you don't!' he said, his voice rising, a catch

in it. 'If you did want to, you would have stayed, you would have told me then. But you didn't want me.'

'I did want you, Jeremiah,' Nick said hoarsely. 'I do want you—more than you can ever imagine. But I didn't think you'd want me. The man you've always thought was your father was a hero, a brave man. How could I be as good as that?'

He stopped abruptly, turning to the window and propping his hand on the frame, staring out into the courtyard. Kate could see the muscles working in his jaw, see the tears tracking down his cheek, and she reached out a hand and laid it against his side in comfort. He closed his eyes and swallowed, and she dropped her hand and turned back to her son.

'Don't blame him, Jem,' she said softly. 'It was me who lied to you, me who let you believe my husband was your father. And Nick didn't know. I didn't tell him for ages, because of Auntie Annabel. It wouldn't have been fair to her. He's only known for two years.'

'So why didn't you tell him before? After Auntie Annabel died, why didn't you tell him then? You could have told him then,' he said, his voice accusing.

'I didn't know how,' she said softly. 'He was very sad and angry when she died, and he was very busy at work sorting out the practice. It wouldn't have been a good time. There was never a good time. I thought there would be, I kept waiting, but then—when he did know—'

'I tried,' Nick said, turning back from the window again, his face taut. 'It may not seem like it, but I did try. But James was a hard act to follow. I thought maybe you'd be happier with things as they were, with me just as Uncle Nick, just as I've always been. And I tried to spend more time with you, quality time, to get to know you and let you get to know me, and I thought we might be getting somewhere, but then that woman commented on us looking alike, and I panicked. I wasn't sure the time was right, and I was so worried I'd make it worse. And just when I thought we ought to try again, your mother met Rob, and they seemed to be getting on so well. He's a good man, and I thought he'd make you a good father, a much better father than I would. You all seemed to be so happy together, and I didn't feel I had the right to destroy that. What good would it have done, Jem? I could have ruined it for you, for all of you. I didn't want to do that. I didn't have the right—'

'But you're my real father,' Jem sobbed, his bruised face anguished. 'You should have told me! I should have known.' I don't care if you're complete rubbish. It's better than being dead!' And he turned his face into the pillow and sobbed brokenly.

Kate leant forwards, resting a hand on his shoulder, but he shrugged her off, and she bit her lip and tried to stop the tears, but they fell anyway, coursing down her cheeks and dripping off her chin, and then she felt Nick's arms round her, cradling her gently against his side as he perched on the arm of the chair.

'Shh. Come on, he'll be all right,' he murmured, his voice ragged. 'He'll come round.'

'No, I won't,' Jem sobbed from the depths of the pillow. 'I won't be all right. Leave me alone! I hate you both! Go away!'

And then she felt Nick shudder, felt the pain tearing through him, and she slid her arms around his waist and hung on.

'Come on, let's give him some space,' he muttered after a few seconds, but she wouldn't leave him.

'I can't go. Not now. You go, leave me with him. I'll talk to him.'

'Will you be all right?'

She lifted her tear-stained face to him and tried to smile. 'I'll have to be, won't I? I have to do this, Nick. He's my son.'

A tremor ran through him, and he stood up. 'I'll see you later—I'll give you an hour. Call me if you need me to come back,' he said, and, closing the curtains around the bed, he walked swiftly away.

She watched him go, listened to the sound of his footsteps retreating, and then she turned back to Jem, biting her lip and wondering how on earth she could unravel this sorry mess of hurt and lies and broken trust that they'd created.

She had no idea. She just knew she had to find a way.

Tentatively, with nothing but love on her side, she reached out her hand and touched him.

'I'm sorry. I'm so, so sorry,' she said unsteadily, and after a moment he opened his eyes and turned his head to look at her.

'Why?' he asked, his voice breaking. 'Why didn't you tell me? I could have kept a secret.

All these years, I thought I didn't have a dad, that I'd never have a dad. And then you met Rob, and I thought maybe he could be my stepdad, but all the time I had a real father, and I didn't know!'

'I know. But you do at least know him, even if you didn't realise he was your father. I've made sure you see him regularly, and he knows you, and all about you. I did everything I could under the circumstances. Don't blame him, Jem. It was my fault, too, and he didn't have any choice. I kept it from him too. And I'm so sorry we've hurt you.'

He sniffed, but the tears still welled, and, unable to bear it, she got up and leant over, taking him gently into her arms, and he burrowed his face into the side of her neck.

Nick held it together just long enough to get out of St Piran, and then he pulled over on the coast road into a parking area, got out of the car and sucked in a lungful of the fresh, salt air.

If he'd been that sort of man, he could have wept bitter, anguished tears for the son he'd let down and all the years that had been lost. Years he couldn't give him back, years that were gone for ever. But he wasn't, and so he shoved it all aside and concentrated his efforts on the future.

If it took him till the end of his life, he vowed, he'd do his best to build a relationship with this child.

He got back in the car and drove to his house. There were some things he needed to pick up, and he could be alone there, think things through.

Except he wasn't alone. Sam Cavendish was there, just coming out of his mother's house next door, and he propped himself against the fence and frowned at Nick.

'You look like hell. Fancy a drink?'

'No, I'm going back to the hospital. We just told him.'

Sam winced sympathetically. 'Ouch. How did it go?'

'Pretty much as expected. Why don't you come in? I don't really want to talk about it here.'

So Sam followed him into the house and propped himself up on the worktop while Nick put the kettle on, for something to do as much as anything.

'So—what happened?' Sam prompted.

Nick sighed and rammed a hand through his hair. 'There was a kid in there having a blood transfusion, and Jem was asking about where his own blood transfusion had come from, and it sort of followed from there. He's the same blood group as me.'

'Yeah, Jack told me,' Sam said. 'And how did he take it?'

'Badly. He's angry. He said he'd spent nearly eleven years thinking he didn't have a father, and all the time he did, and he said...' His voice cracked, and he coughed again and flexed his fingers. 'He said he didn't care if I was complete rubbish, it was better than being dead.'

Sam snorted. 'Well, I'd agree with him if my own wasn't so useless he might as well be dead, but what made him think you'd be rubbish?'

'I did. I told him James was a hard act to follow, that he might have preferred a hero. Apparently not. I didn't realise Jack had told you about the blood group thing.'

'Mmm. He was angry, but he's not really surprised.'

Nick's head snapped up and he stared at Sam, stunned. 'What makes you say that?'

Sam laughed softly. 'Oh, come on, Nick, everyone knows you've always loved Kate.'

They did? Well, why the hell hadn't they all

reminded him of that in Freshers' Week when he'd been busy drinking himself senseless and making love to the first pretty girl who'd had enough alcohol to make her forget her common sense and sleep with him—the pretty girl who'd told him four weeks later that she was pregnant, and nine months later had presented him with twins, and then a year later with another son, while he'd worked his way through university supported by their parents and tried not to think about the girl he'd left behind. Had Annabel known she wasn't his first choice? Had she known he'd only done the decent thing and made the best marriage he could with the hand fate had dealt him? He sincerely hoped not, but if his feelings had been so obvious to everyone else, then why not to her?

And she'd sent him into Kate's arms, the night of the storm, almost as if she'd known that only Kate could comfort him.

'I tried to love her,' he murmured, as much to himself as to Sam, then he lifted his head and met Sam's eyes. 'I did love her, and I tried to be a good husband, and I think we had a good marriage, but maybe I was deluding myself.'

'I don't think so. I remember her—I grew up next door, don't forget. I spent a lot of time in this house. It was like a second home to me at one point. And she always seemed very happy, contented. At peace. She had a good life with you and a lovely family. I don't think you let her down, Nick. And she's been gone five years now. I think if anything you let yourself down, cheated yourself, and Kate, for too long. And maybe now it's time to do something positive about that.'

Sam shrugged away from the worktop, clapped Nick on the shoulder and headed for the front door. 'I'm going home to my wife and child. And tomorrow we're going house-hunting.'

Nick followed him through to the hall.

'Why?'

Sam laughed. 'Because my ankle doesn't like the hill and Gemma can't lift the buggy up the steps into the house. And we need to be nearer my mother.'

'How much nearer?' he asked, an idea dawning. 'Like—next door?'

Sam's eyes narrowed and he tilted his head on one side. 'Next door? As in, here?'

He nodded. 'There's a barn. I've just moved into it with Kate, so that when Jem comes out of the hospital in a few days he can live on the flat for a bit until he's got his mobility back—assuming he's speaking to us by then. And it's for sale. We're renting it at the moment, but I think it's time to move on, time to lay Annabel's ghost to rest, whatever happens with me and Kate and Jeremiah. So I'm going to sell this house, and buy the barn, and then if it works out...'

Sam's jaw sagged slightly, and then he laughed. 'Really? You're selling? How much?'

He shrugged. 'I have no idea. It's the least of my worries. I won't cheat you, Sam.'

Sam grinned. 'I'll make sure of it. Talk to the agents—let me know. And I'll go and sound Gemma out, but I know what she'll say. She loves this house, and so do I.'

Nick felt himself smile as the weight lifted a little. 'I know you do,' he said. 'And it needs another family.'

And if Sam and Gemma bought it from him, it would bring his dream a little closer...

CHAPTER NINE

HE FOUND Kate in the deserted café, sitting nursing a stale cup of coffee and looking like death.

He sat down opposite her and took the cup out of her hands. It was stone cold, and he tutted softly and wrapped her hands in his to warm them. 'How is he?'

She shrugged. 'They had to give him some more morphine and something to help him sleep. I think it was all the upset...'

She trailed off, and he sighed, stroking his thumb over the back of her hand. 'What did he say? After I left.'

She shrugged again, a helpless little gesture that made his heart ache for her. 'He's just really shocked, I think. It's a lot for him to take in. I explained to the staff—the night sister and Megan Phillips. They were really nice to him. Megan, especially, was really lovely. She's such a nice girl. And I rang Jess Carmichael, and she came up and talked to me for a minute while he was asleep, and she makes so much sense. She's going to come and see him when he's feeling a little better and let him talk it through with her.'

'Do you think he will?' Nick asked, not sure about the idea of unburdening to a counsellor, but Kate nodded.

'I think so. He likes her. He talked to her before, when I was ill.' She sighed. 'Nick, I'm really tired, can you take me home?' she asked, and his heart contracted.

'Sure,' he said softly, and, helping her to her feet, he wrapped an arm round her shoulders and led her out to the car.

'So much for Ben's chilli,' she said as they went into the house, and he just pulled her into his arms and held her while the dog sniffed and wagged around their feet. She was exhausted, and she had to be hungry. He was—or his body was. His heart wasn't in the least bit interested in anything as trivial as food, but for her sake, he'd fix them something to eat and make sure she ate it.

'I'll cook us something quick,' he said, giving her a last little hug and letting her go. 'We can have more of the cold pie, or toast, or anything you want.'

'Toast,' she said. 'Toast and a nice, hot cup

of tea. And it's cold—I know it's April, but do you think it would be possible to put the heating on?'

'Want me to light the fire?'

She glanced at the big woodburner and sighed longingly. 'Oh, that would be lovely. Is there any wood?'

He nodded. 'There's a pile out in the cart lodge, I'll get some while I'm taking the dog out. I'll put the kettle on, you go and sit down. You look done in.'

'Do you think we could have done things any differently?' she asked later, as they lay side by side with their legs stretched out towards the fire and its living hearthrug.

Nick stared at the dog and wondered what it must be like to have no responsibilities. 'In what way?' he asked. 'Do you mean the way we told him now, or if we should have told him years ago? Either way, I don't know. I don't think there was a right way, under the circumstances, but I wish you'd told me sooner, Kate. I wish I'd known, right back at the beginning. I would have made sure I saw more of him.'

'How?' she asked, turning her head to face

him, searching his eyes and finding only confusion that mirrored her own. 'You were working in Wadebridge, living in Penhally, and I can
see your house from mine—I could look across
sometimes and see Annabel hanging the washing out! How were you going to spend time with
him, under those circumstances, without arousing
suspicion? And I didn't want to do that to you, to
put you under that sort of pressure for something
that hadn't been your fault.'

'Of course it was my fault!' he said. 'I heard
you crying and I walked in when I knew you were
naked, when I'd seen you, I'd undressed you—
dammit, Kate, I knew what was going to happen
if I opened that door.'

'Nick, I was falling apart, and so were you.' She
lifted her hand and cradled his jaw, feeling the
muscles clench beneath her palm. 'You needed
me, every bit as much as I needed you. We were
on autopilot—we didn't set out to make love, and
if I hadn't got pregnant, nobody would ever have
known.'

'I would have known. I never forgot, Kate. It
haunted me—it still haunts me. And things with
Annabel were never quite the same after that.
I don't really know why, if it was because I'd

changed, or because she sensed what happened between us that night. Maybe she even knew Jem was mine. I'll never know. But I knew when I walked through that door how dangerous it was, and I should have stopped myself.'

'And left me there alone, in that state? How was that right?' She leant over, closing the gap and touching her lips lightly to his cheek, then rested her head on his shoulder. 'I needed you, Nick, and you needed me, more than we'd ever needed anyone before. It wasn't your fault, it was just one of those things—part of being human. And you can't take all the responsibility for the fact that I got pregnant.'

'Why not? I know how the system works, Kate, and God knows I'd had enough object lessons in it!'

She eased back so she could look at him. 'Was Annabel on the Pill?'

'Yes.'

'So it wasn't unreasonable that you didn't think about contraception, because it wasn't a normal part of your sex life at the time. Nor was it mine. I didn't even think about it. James and I had been trying for three years, and we'd finally admitted that there might be something wrong and gone for tests, just a week before. We were still waiting for the results when he died, and maybe I should have told you, but how? Who would have gained?'

He sighed, and his arm around her back tightened a fraction and eased her closer.

'You're right,' he murmured as she rested her head back on his shoulder. 'It was an impossible decision, a no-win situation. There was no right way to deal with it, we've just got to make sure we do it right now. Maybe you'd better give me a script.'

'You don't need a script. Just rely on your instincts, Nick.'

'My instincts are fatally flawed,' he said drily. 'If we rely on them, it's a sure-fire recipe for disaster. And talking of my instincts, before I do anything else I'll regret, I'm going to take the dog out, and then I'm going to bed.'

She tilted her head and stared up into his eyes, held motionless by the sensual message in their rich chocolate depths, and with a ragged sigh he eased her closer and touched his mouth to hers.

She parted her lips, and he growled low in his throat and took instant advantage, the hot, silken sweep of his tongue plundering her mouth, sliding one hand around the back of her neck and threading his fingers through her hair to steady her as the other hand curled around her bottom and hauled her closer. Her legs parted at the pressure from his knee, and one hard thigh lodged between them, sending need shooting through her, turning her body to fire.

'Nick,' she moaned, but the sound of her voice seemed to stop him in his tracks, and he pulled back, lifting his head and staring down at her, his chest rising and falling rapidly. She could see the hammer of his heartbeat in the hollow of his throat, and after an endless moment he got to his feet and walked away, calling the dog.

'Nick?'

'Leave it, Kate. For the love of God, just leave it,' he said rawly, and she heard the door shut behind him, the lights coming on automatically as he walked out of the back door from the utility room into the garden, the dog at his heels.

For an age she sat there, staring after him, her eyes fixed blindly on the closed door, and then with a fractured little sigh she got to her feet, put their glasses in the kitchen and went to bed.

They were supposed to be being grown up about this, she reminded herself, and so far it was only Nick who was sticking to the plot. How long that would last, she had no idea, but as she lay down in her bed, her mind went back to Jem.

How on earth had she forgotten about him? He was lying there in hospital, distressed and heartbroken, and all she could think about was making love with Nick, which was what had got them all in this mess in the first place!

It was a long, long time before she went to sleep.

The next day was very hard.

Jem refused to talk to Kate at first, and he refused to let Nick visit. After he'd got over his crying spell the night before, he'd withdrawn into himself, and the only thing he showed any interest in was Lucy's games console. It took him out of himself, she thought, gave him something to concentrate on, something to hide behind while his subconscious sorted out the wood from the trees.

So she just sat beside him, reading a magazine and waiting, and finally he cracked.

'Why did you lie to me?' he asked suddenly, and she put her magazine down and made herself meet his hurt, accusing eyes.

'I didn't—well, not really. I tried very hard not

to, and I never actually told you that James was your father, because I knew it was a lie, and it was more a case of letting you believe something than telling you something wrong. So when you asked about your father, I told you that if he'd known he had a son, he would have been very proud of you, and that, at least, is true. He is proud of you, and he loves you. He always has.'

'But you let me think that James was my father. That was a sort of lie.'

It was. A lie of omission, and she nodded. 'Yes, it was. But it seemed like the best of some not very good choices, and I wanted to do the best I could for everyone. I didn't really know what else to do without hurting innocent people.'

'I'm innocent,' he said, and her eyes filled.

'I know. I'm sorry. It's a mess, and it's my fault, not your father's. You shouldn't blame him, he had no say in it.'

'Where is Uncle N—?' he asked, and then frowned. 'Mum, what do I call him now?' he asked fretfully.

She stroked his hair. 'I don't know. You'll have to ask him that. Whatever feels right. What do you want to call him?'

He shrugged. 'Dunno. I mean, he's my dad, isn't he?'

She nodded, blinking back the ever-ready tears. 'Yes. Yes, he is, but you must do what feels right for you both. I can't tell you that, darling, it's up to you. And he's here—I expect he's in the café. Why? Do you want to see him now?'

He shrugged his skinny shoulders again. 'Just wondered if he'd gone. He went home yesterday.'

'Because you told him to.'

'But I didn't think he'd go,' he said perversely. 'Not if he really cared.'

'Oh, he cares, Jem,' she said softly. 'He was really upset. He went because you asked him to, not because he wanted to, and that's why he's not here now, but he is in the hospital, in case you want to see him. And he'll be here, waiting, until you're ready.'

'Really?'

She nodded. 'Really. However long it takes. He wants to see you,' she told him, and she watched that sink in, watched the realisation that Nick did care, that he wanted Jem. Was here for him, any time he asked.

He didn't ask, not then, but later, when he'd

obviously been thinking about it for a while, he lifted his head and said, 'This face-merging thing. Do you think it would work with him and me?'

She took a second to realise he was talking about the games console, and lifted her shoulders. 'I don't know. Probably. Do you want to try?'

'Maybe. If he's still here.'

She felt a great weight lift off her chest, and smiled. 'I'll find him.'

He was in the café, in a litter of torn sugar and salt packets, pushing a pile of white crystals around on the tabletop.

She sat down next to him, and he lifted his head and gave her a weary smile. 'Hi. How is he?'

'He's OK. He wants to see you.'

His eyes widened, and she could see hope flickering in them. 'Really?'

'Really. He was talking about the photo-merging thing. I think he wants to try with your faces.'

'Ah. That might need Jack or Lucy.'

'It might not. You might be able to work it out. You've got the instructions.'

He nodded slowly. 'I could try. Any tips or hints? For him, not the game.'

'Give him time. He's still angry with us, but

more than that, he's confused and he needs time to adjust to the new reality of having a father. We all need time to adjust to it, but we'll get there.'

'Will we?' he asked doubtfully, as they left the café and walked along to the ward. 'I hope you're right.'

She sent him in on his own, and Jem looked up and gave him a wary smile.

He smiled back just as warily and sat down on the chair. 'Hiya. Your mum says you want to try the face-merging thing.'

'Mmm.' Jem fiddled with the games console for a moment, then mumbled, 'Uncle Nick? Can I call you Dad? 'Cos that's what you are, really, and it's what Jack and Lucy call you. But I'm still mad with you, though, for walking off and not explaining,' he added hastily, just in case he wasn't aware of it.

No chance of that. Nick's throat closed, and he swallowed hard. 'That's fine, I deserve it. You can call me whatever you want. And if you want to call me Dad—well, that would be awesome.'

His son rolled his eyes and grinned, looking so like Jack that Nick couldn't believe he'd never seen it. 'You can't say that, Dad, you're too old, you sound silly. And I am still mad with you.'

He gave him a wry smile. 'That's OK. We can talk about that,' he agreed, and blinked hard. He'd called him Dad—as if he'd been practising it in his head all day, and finally felt brave enough to try it out. Brave enough, and trusting enough.

He sucked in a deep breath, and picked up the games console. 'Right. Instructions?'

'They're here. Where's Mum?'

'I think she's having a drink and a bit of fresh air. Why?'

He shrugged. 'Just wondered. I thought she'd like to see this.'

'We can show her later when she comes back, if we can work it out. Or I can go outside and phone her,' Nick suggested, realising Jem was still scared. Still scared, and still needing his mother, but the man who'd been Uncle Nick all his life didn't have the power to fill that gap, and maybe never would. He realised that he was jealous of her relationship with him. So stupid. Of course he needed his mother, he was a little boy, still not quite eleven years old, for all his courage.

'Want me to call her? She could come now, I'm sure. She's not far away.'

Jem shook his head. 'No, it's OK. We can show her later, like you said,' he agreed, and Nick felt himself relax a little. One step at a time…

'We did it, Mum, it was amazing,' their son said by way of greeting, and she felt the tension ease out of her.

'Did you make it work, then?' she asked him, and he nodded.

'Yeah—come here, let me show you. And I'm going to look so like him when I'm older. It's awesome, isn't it, Dad?' he said, and Kate's eyes widened slightly and then filled with tears.

'Yes, you will be like him,' she said, looking at the games console as Jem switched from one face to another, the similarities striking. Her voice wobbled slightly, and she swallowed hard and avoided Nick's eyes. But he'd seen, and his hand came out and squeezed hers in support.

'Lucy sent me a text. She's invited us for supper. Want to go?'

She shook her head. 'No. I ought to let the dog out and I could do with putting some washing on before I come back here this evening, but you can go, if you like.'

'No. That's fine. I'll drop in and have a cup of

tea with her after I take you home, and I could go and pick up my post—yours, too.'

'You can go now, Dad, if you like,' Jem said. 'Mum and me'll be all right.'

'Mum and I,' she corrected automatically, and turned in time to see the flicker of pain on Nick's face.

'Sure. I'll do the dog and the post and have tea with Lucy, and I'll come back this evening and take you home after visiting, then, if you're both sure?' Nick said gruffly, and then, after a fractional hesitation, he bent over the bed and dropped a kiss on his son's bruised forehead. Just a fleeting one, the sort of kiss he'd given his other boys in their youth, but he wasn't sure of his reception and when Jem slid his arms round him and gave him a quick hug, he felt the love swell in his chest and threaten to choke him.

'You take care,' he said gruffly, ruffling his hair with a gentle hand, and because he didn't want to leave her out, he stooped and kissed Kate's cheek, as well, in passing, and he was rewarded by her smile.

At least supper was sorted out, he thought as he headed back to Lucy's—fresh sea bass from one of the fishermen in the harbour. He'd been spotted turning into his drive when he'd collected his post, and Toby Penhaligan had pulled in behind him and given him two beautiful, plump fish straight from the sea.

'How's the lad?' he'd asked, and Nick wondered if he'd heard the rumour, too.

'Doing well, thanks,' he'd told him. 'He should be out of hospital by the end of next week.'

'I hear you've taken the barn for the summer.'

So the jungle drums were working overtime. No surprises there, then. 'For a while, anyway. I'm giving Kate a hand to look after Jem—he can't manage the stairs, so it seemed to make sense.'

He'd felt Toby's eyes track to the more-than-adequate family house behind him, and was hugely grateful that the barn was out of the way and might afford them a little much-needed privacy.

He'd gone straight there, put the fish in the fridge and walked the dog, then gone to Lucy's.

'So, how is he?' she asked.

'OK,' he told them. 'Good. He called me Dad today...'

His voice cracked a bit, and he cleared his throat and gave them a wry smile. They were gathered round the kitchen table, his two eldest children and Ben, drinking tea and talking through Jem's progress, and Lucy reached out a hand and squeezed his shoulder. 'Sorry,' he muttered, patting her hand. 'It got to me. But he says he's still mad with me. He thinks I don't want to be his father.'

'Do you?' Jack asked. 'Because I could understand if you didn't. I was appalled when India died and I was told Freddie was mine—talk about hurled in at the deep end. It really wasn't easy, but you've got to give it a go, Dad, because— well, he's the best thing that's ever happened to mc, him and Alison and our growing family. But it was Freddie that turned me around, and he's given me so much.'

'I'm sure you're the best thing that's ever happened to him, as well. And I do want to be his father. I just hope I can do him justice.'

'Of course you can! It's not about being perfect, it's about being there,' Lucy told him. 'And listening. You could maybe do a bit more of that. But we were never short of love, and that's what he needs most of all. To know you love him.'

'I do.' He swallowed and tried to smile. 'He hugged me. When I said goodbye. He's never hugged me before.'

Lucy tutted again, and got up and came round and snuggled onto his lap. 'You soft old thing,' she said kindly, and he laughed and tapped her on the bottom.

'Less of the old,' he told her, and hugged her back, then frowned and looked down at her slightly rounded abdomen. 'Are you pregnant again?'

She blushed. 'Um—I might be.'

'I think you might. Congratulations. I take it this is planned?'

Ben's lips twitched. 'Sort of. She caught me in a weak moment. I think it's a ploy to be on permanent maternity leave.'

Nick laughed again. 'Come on, let me up. I have to go and see your little brother.'

Jem was tired—exhausted, really, after a busy day with two lots of visitors and all the upset of the previous day—and he was still getting used to being out in an open ward with six-bed bays, rather than his own quiet little side room, so Kate and Nick didn't stay late, and were home by quarter to eight.

Home, he thought, turning into the drive, and

wondered how, in just a little over forty-eight hours, it could possibly feel like home.

Because Kate was there.

There was no other possible reason, and he ushered her in, poured her a glass of wine while she let the dog out and fussed over him, then scrubbed the new potatoes while she sat and sipped the wine and watched the last pink streaks of the sunset fade over the sea.

'Anything I can do?' she asked him, feeling guilty for sitting there, but he just smiled at her and carried on scraping and scrubbing.

'No. You stay there and enjoy being waited on. You heard the doctor—I have to spoil you.'

She chuckled. 'If you insist. So how was Lucy?'

'Ah, Lucy. Pregnant again.'

Kate smiled indulgently. 'Have you only just realised?' she said.

He rolled his eyes. 'Of course, you're a midwife. You notice these things.'

'That's right,' she said smugly. 'So, what are you feeding me for supper?' she asked, and he grinned.

'Sea bass, courtesy of Toby Penhaligan.'

'Sea bass? Really? Are you going to make

the house smell of fish?' she queried, and he laughed.

'I shouldn't think so, the extractor fan's like a jet engine, I'll be surprised if it doesn't suck the fish out of the pan. I tell you what, while I do this, why don't you go and have a shower?'

'Do you mind?'

'Not at all. Consider it all part of your pampering,' he said, and his eyes raked slowly over her and he smiled. 'You could even wear something pretty.'

Pretty? Her heart thudded, and she felt a sudden flutter of nerves. He was looking at her as if…

Oh, lord. She wasn't ready for this. Last night she had been, but tonight, just like that, without the benefit of cuddling up to him and getting in the mood, she felt a shiver of ice slide down her spine. Nick wasn't coy, and he wouldn't be a shy lover. He'd want the lights on and access to every part of her, and she wasn't sure she could do this. Not now, and maybe not ever.

'I'll see what I've got. It might just be jumper and jeans,' she said, and headed for her bedroom, panic clawing at her throat.

He put the potatoes in the pan and glanced at his watch. She might be half an hour in the shower and then getting ready, so he had time to light the fire to give it time to warm up the room.

He brought some wood in, and while he was laying the fire, he heard a noise coming from the area of her bedroom.

'Kate?'

He walked down the corridor towards her room, and heard the shower running, and then a muffled sob.

He rested his head against the door. Not again. He couldn't do this again.

So he went into her room and stood by the window, staring out into the courtyard and listening in agony as she wept just feet away from him. There was nothing he could do—nothing he would let himself do—but wait until the crying stopped, and a minute later she turned off the water, then he heard the door open and she walked into the room, closing the door and then dropping her towel.

And then she saw him, and gasped, scrabbling for the towel, her eyes red-rimmed and wild with some unfathomable emotion.

He reached for her, shocked at the ravaged look on her face, the pain in her eyes, desperate to comfort her, but she wouldn't let him.

'Nick, no,' she said, pushing him away and trying to turn her back to him, the towel twisted somehow round her now. 'Please!'

'Don't be silly, I've seen you cry umpteen times in the last few days,' he said gently, his hands cupping her shoulders, but she shook her head.

'No—it's not that. Please, Nick, just go—'

She broke off, the smothered sobs returning, and he felt swamped by her pain, the light slowly dawning as he realised belatedly why she'd turned away.

'Oh, my love, my darling girl, come here,' he said tenderly, turning her back into his arms and folding her against his chest once more, his hands stroking her back rhythmically through the damp towel. 'After all we've been through, do you really think a few scars are going to make any difference to me?'

'They make a difference to me,' she sobbed, pushing him away again, but he wouldn't let her go this time, he couldn't, because the pain and fear for her, suppressed for nearly a year now, were rising up and choking him, and he cradled her tenderly against his heart and rocked her. Rocked them both.

'I thought you were going to die,' he said

unevenly. 'I thought I was going to lose you, lose everything that kept me sane. You're my best friend, Kate, the one person who really understands me; the only thing that's kept me going is working with you, having you there near me, even if you weren't with me. I prayed so hard that you'd make it, even if you ended up with Rob—that didn't matter, just so long as you were alive, just so long as I knew you were somewhere in the world. Why the hell should I care about a scar?'

'Oh, Nick,' she whispered tearfully, and, resting her head against his shoulder, she slid her arms round him and held him. 'I'm sorry. I didn't even think about how you might have felt, just that you hadn't been there for me, but nobody was there for you. I'm so, so sorry.'

She breathed deeply, then looked at him again. 'It's just— Nobody's seen it, and when you said wear something pretty, I felt ridiculously shy all of a sudden, and I thought, what if it turned you off?'

'Kate!' he chided softly, gutted that she thought so little of him. 'How shallow do you think I am?'

'I don't. It's how shallow I am.'

He gave a ragged sigh and cradled her head against his shoulder. 'Can we start again? Wear something that makes you feel good. Something that makes you feel all woman, because you are, Kate. You're a beautiful woman, and I want to show you that, but only when you're ready. There's no pressure. I don't care if it takes months. Years. I want you, and I'll wait for you.'

She sucked in a breath and took a little step back. 'I'll see what I can find. Why don't you go and start cooking?'

CHAPTER TEN

'ANYTHING I can do?'

He lifted his head and smiled at her, but he didn't comment on her clothes, and she felt perversely irritated. 'You could top and tail the mangetout, if you're bored. And you look lovely, by the way. Beautiful.'

The irritation dissolved in an instant, replaced by a rush of heat and affection for this complicated and loveable man. He brought her the packet of peas, a pan and a small knife, dropped a tender, lingering kiss on her lips, and she sat at the table with a silly smile and trimmed the peas and sipped another glass of wine while he put the fish on to cook and prodded the potatoes. Music was playing in the background, something soft and smoky and sensual, and between that and the wine and the last streaks of the sunset fading into the night, it was the perfect romantic setting.

All she needed was her son back home, safe and sound, and her happiness would be complete.

Once she'd found the courage to make love to Nick, at least.

Did he feel the same way about it? She glanced across at him, and saw he was humming softly as he worked. He looked happy enough. It was lovely to be able to sit there and enjoy all of the house without moving, she thought, and told herself it could be permanent, that they could stay there and make it their home.

'Right, let's have those peas. How's your wine?'

'It's fine. I don't need any more. I'm still on the occasional anti-inflammatory and I don't like to mix drugs and alcohol.'

'I thought that was what the modern youth did.'

'It is. I'm not the modern youth.'

'I'm thankful for that.'

They shared a smile, and then with a shake of his head, as if he was collecting himself, he turned back to his cooking and the moment was gone.

'That was gorgeous, Nick. Thank you.'

'My pleasure. It was worth being grilled by

Toby Penhaligan to get those sea bass. They were gorgeous.'

'Did he give you a very hard time?'

Nick shrugged. 'The jungle drums are obviously working, but I suppose we should expect that. I think we need to present a united front, for Jem's sake, and if the gossip gets too much—well, who knows what the future might hold?'

His words hung in the air, and Kate met his eyes and saw a hope in them that must surely be reflected in her own. She wanted him. She wanted to be with him, to spend her life with him, and their son did, too.

And to do that, she had to find the courage to do what she had to do next.

'Nick? Will you do something for me?'

'Sure. What is it?'

'Will you make love to me?'

He froze, his glass suspended above the table, and after what seemed like for ever he set it back down very, very carefully and uncurled his fingers from the stem.

'Are you sure?' he asked hoarsely.

'Yes. Yes, I'm sure, but I'm scared.'

'Oh, Kate…'

He stood up and came round to her side, taking

her hands in his. 'You don't have to be scared. This is me. Why on earth are you scared?'

'Because—I just am. It's been a long time, Nick. And—well, I don't look the same.'

'You know what I feel about that,' he said.

'But it's not only about what you feel, it's about what I feel, and I feel—I know it's stupid, I know it's irrational, I've seen lots of women who've had breast surgery, but they weren't me. This is me, my body, and that makes it different. And illogical,' she explained, and he frowned slightly and squeezed her hand.

'I can understand that, but, Kate, I could have lost you, but I didn't. You're here with me, now, and that, at the end, is the only thing that matters. That you're alive and well.'

'And then there's the competition,' she went on, ignoring him. 'I'm not Annabel,' she said, pointing out the obvious. 'Or any one of the other glamorous women you've been seen with.'

He sighed and shifted to the chair beside her, lifting her hand and pressing it to his cheek. 'I know you're not Annabel,' he said gently. 'You don't have to live up to her, Kate. I loved her, just not the way I've always loved you. You were always my soul mate. You were the one I should have been with all this time. She was a lovely girl, and she turned into a kind, sensitive and generous woman; as a mother, I couldn't fault her. As a wife, she was perfect. We were good friends in many ways, but there was no great passion there, no desperate yearning. And as for the other women—there's only really been one since Annabel, and she has no expectations. I've seen her from time to time. Her name's Louise. We've had dinner, gone to the cinema.'

'Made love?'

'I'm not a monk, Kate. Neither am I promiscuous. The others have just been passing distractions, but I haven't slept with them. And I'm not going to beat you up about Rob.'

'What makes you think I slept with him?'

He shook his head and gave a wry smile. 'I saw you. I came to see you, last summer. I wanted to talk to you, and I pulled up outside. And Rob was kissing you, in the kitchen, right in front of the window. And then you walked away, and a light came on upstairs, and you shut the bedroom curtains. It wasn't rocket science, Kate.'

She felt sick. 'Nick, you weren't meant to see that.'

'Of course not. But you're adults, so why not?

After all, we weren't going anywhere, were we, at the time, and he's a good guy. So—why not? It's what people do. I know that. And I can understand it, but it's all very well in theory, but in practice, I realised I was jealous.'

'Because even though you didn't want me, you didn't want anyone else to?'

'But I did want you. I just didn't know how to ask. I went to see Louise, after I drove away that night. I thought—what was sauce for the goose, I suppose. But, well, let's just say I think I was a bit of a disappointment to her. I couldn't get you out of my head, couldn't stop seeing you kissing him, and I didn't want to be with her. I didn't want to be with anyone if I couldn't be with you, and obviously I couldn't. So I went home, picked up a bottle of Scotch from the kitchen, walked down to the beach and drank half of it. I haven't seen her since.'

'So who was the woman at Ben and Lucy's barbecue last summer?' she asked.

'An old friend from London. She's divorced, she was down here on holiday, and she was lonely.'

Kate smiled indulgently. 'I think she was probably more than lonely, the way she was looking at you.'

He shrugged. 'I'm a good-looking guy—what can I say?' he murmured, and she laughed, as he'd meant her to. But then his smile faded, and he lifted his hand and touched her cheek. 'She was nothing, Kate. Nothing happened with her, I promise. I can't dismiss Annabel, she was my wife, the mother of three of my children, a very important person in our lives, and I loved her. But there truly has been no one else who matters at all, no one who's ever claimed my heart or made me want to behave like an irrational teenager or a romantic fool. No one else who's been such a good friend to me no matter how badly I've behaved. No one else that I've loved the way I love you. The way I've always loved you.'

'Oh, Nick. What happened to us?' she asked softly, and he stood up slowly and drew her to her feet.

'I don't know. I just know that now we seem to have a chance, and I want to take that chance with you, Kate. Let me try again,' he murmured softly. 'I know I don't deserve it, but give me a chance to prove that I can be a good husband and father. We're stuck with each other for good now, anyway, as Jem's parents—why not do it properly? There's so much at stake here now—so much that's infinitely precious that I really don't think I can bear to lose.'

Her mouth dropped open slightly, and she stared at him in confusion. 'Are you—? Did I imagine it, or did you just ask me to marry you?'

He felt emotion choke him, and swallowed. 'I'm not sure. I think I might have done, but not just because of Jem. I can be a father to him whatever, if I get the chance, and that's down to him. And if he hates me, if he wants me out of his life...'

'He doesn't. He won't.'

'Then give me a chance, Kate. Let's wind back the clock and start again, only as adults with hopefully a bit more judgement and common sense and compassion. See if we can make it work this time.'

She studied him doubtfully. 'Do you think we can do that?'

'I think we can try.'

'Maybe.'

'Is that a maybe maybe, or a definite maybe?' he asked, sure his smile didn't reach his eyes because her answer was so important to him.

'I think that's a definite maybe,' she said, her smile slow, and he felt the tension drain out of him. And then ratchet up again another gear. He lifted his hand and grazed his knuckles gently against her cheek.

'I want to make love to you,' he murmured, 'but I want you to be sure that you're ready for this, because if you're going to change your mind, I'd rather you did it now.'

She gave a quiet sigh. 'The only thing that would change my mind is Jem, and he seems to love you. He's always been very fond of you, and now, knowing you're his father just seems to be strengthening that bond. So, no, I'm not going to change my mind, Nick. But I am still scared.'

He drew her into his arms and cradled her against his heart. 'Don't be scared, my love. I'll take care of you. I'll always take care of you.'

He let her go, then took her hand and led her slowly and carefully up the stairs to his room, closing the door behind them just in case Bruno decided to follow them, but he was lying on a rug chasing rabbits in his sleep, and she didn't think he'd worry.

'Do you want the lights off?' he asked, and she swallowed.

She had to do this. She had to be brave enough to show herself to him, to open up all her physical and emotional scars to him and trust him to heal them. But the lights…

'How about the bathroom light? We could leave the door open,' he suggested, and she nodded, ridiculously nervous now.

He turned back the bed, stripped off his clothes down to his boxers—jersey boxers that fitted snugly over his firm, muscular buttocks and thighs and did heart-stopping things in other areas—and then held out his hand to her.

She went to his side, and he stared down at her, his eyes sombre. 'Are you sure, Kate?' he said softly. 'We've had years to talk this up in our heads, and I don't want to disappoint you.'

'You won't disappoint me.' She knew he wouldn't. She didn't know how, she just knew. She went up on tiptoe and brushed her lips against his, then dropped back onto her heels and waited.

He unbuttoned the silky blouse she'd put on, the sheer fabric sliding against her skin as he loosened it and slipped it over her shoulders. He laid it carefully on the chair, then his fingers found the zip on her trousers and slid it down, the faint noise loud in the breathless silence. The button was next, and then they joined the blouse on the chair and he stood back and looked at her, standing there in her underwear.

'You're still a really beautiful woman, Kate,' he said softly. 'Come here. I need you.'

He held out his hand, and she put hers in it and went into his arms, closing the gap between them slowly, so that when their bodies touched, it was like coming home.

She rested her head on his shoulder, and he slid his arms round her waist and held her gently against his body, so she could feel the beating of his heart, the rise and fall of his chest as he breathed, the warmth of his skin, and as she lifted her head, his came down and his lips found hers, meshing and melding in a gentle dance that was filled with promise.

She knew he wanted her. She also knew he'd wait for her, give her time for her fears to fade, and it gave her the confidence to step back out of his arms and take off the last of her clothes, so she was standing in front of him naked.

And then she waited.

Her trust was unbearably touching.

He felt his eyes fill with tears, and because he knew she wanted him to, he made himself look down, to study the scar on her left breast, the fine line that ran round underneath it in the crease, the hollow left by the surgery that had saved her life. The skin was a little discoloured from the radiotherapy, but that would fade with time. And it was very neat. The doctor in him admired the surgery. The man wanted her, more than he'd ever wanted any other woman in his life, and if it killed him, he was going to do her justice now.

Her courage humbled him, and he gave her an unsteady smile. 'I feel a little overdressed,' he said gruffly, and skimmed off his boxers, tossing them aside and standing in front of her, wondering how he measured up to Rob and hating himself for caring about something so trivial. Well, at least she could see that he wasn't in the least put off by her appearance. In fact, if she kept him waiting much longer...

'Nick?'

He met her eyes.

'Make love to me.'

He lifted her carefully onto the bed, tutting at the faint bruising on her right foot, touching his lips gently to the little stain. He could imagine her feet trapped in the footwell, knew that if the fuel tank had blown, she would have died.

Don't think about that, he told himself, and moved up, skimming past her thighs, not allowing himself to linger till he reached her waist, then trailing his tongue slowly around her navel, dipping into it, teasing her till she trembled.

Then he moved higher, his hand cupping her left breast, pressing a gentle, healing kiss to the scar. She shuddered a little, and he moved on, his lips sipping and tasting the other breast, reluctant to miss a single inch of her. She moaned and arched up, her body image issues forgotten now, need taking over, the need that had haunted them both for so very many years. The purely sensual need that their one tragic night had never addressed.

He moved up until his face was level with hers, and kissed her as he'd always wanted to kiss her, long and slow and deep—heavy, drugging kisses that cranked up the heat and made his body burn for her.

And hers for him. She plucked at him, her fingers restless, her breathing light and rapid, almost hyperventilating. 'Nick, please…now,' she begged, and doing what he'd failed to do before, taking the time to protect her, he moved over her and thrust slowly, lingeringly home.

She gasped, her body bucking beneath his, and

he locked his mouth to hers, plundering it as he drove into her again and again and again, until at last he could hold it no more and he let himself go, joining her in the long freefall into ecstasy.

The next few days were blissful.

The weather was gorgeous, and when they weren't in the hospital visiting Jem, they were at the barn, sitting under a little ornamental tree in the courtyard garden with the dog at their feet and drinking coffee or sipping wine, and every now and then he'd cook them something wonderful.

And his hidden talent for waiting on her was turning into an art form. He ran errands for her, spoiled her rotten, massaged her neck when it ached and then, when she was boneless and utterly relaxed, he'd make love to her.

They were slow, lazy days, days in which they all recovered from what had been a gruelling ordeal, and gradually they relaxed into a quiet, orderly routine.

He went back to work in the mornings, coming home to cook them lunch before driving to the hospital to visit Jem. He'd settled really well in the new ward, made friends, watched the ducklings grow and gradually, bit by bit, he was getting back on his feet.

Jess Carmichael had been to see him, and he was less angry with his parents, more accepting now that there had been valid reasons why his parentage had been kept from him. 'She's a wonderful person,' Kate said. 'I don't know how I would have coped last year without her. She's a miracle.'

She wasn't the only miracle. Lucy had formed a wonderfully close attachment to Jem, and on a day when Nick was there alone because he'd treated Kate to a pamper break, she brought the children in to see him.

'Hey, you've got the monsters,' Jem said with a grin, and Lucy chuckled.

'Annabel, say hello to Uncle Jem,' she said, letting go of her daughter's hand, and his eyes widened.

'Wow—I really am an uncle, aren't I? That's weird—awesome! Hi, Annabel.'

'We bringed you grapes,' Annabel said, handing him the bag shyly.

'That's because Grandad ate the last lot,' Lucy pointed out with a firm look at her father, and he rolled his eyes.

'Naughty G'andad!' Annabel said, and stared at them longingly.

Jem gave her some, and she settled down on the floor by the window and ate the grapes and counted the ducklings, while Lucy hung onto the baby and tried to keep him out of mischief.

'I can't believe he's a year old,' she said.

'I can't believe I'm a grandfather,' Nick said drily.

Lucy grinned. 'Oh, I can. Look at the grey hairs, Dad! But I can't believe Annabel's nearly two and a half. It seems like five minutes. Joshy, no! You can't have the grapes.'

'Gape!' he yelled, his little fist working, and lunged for them, slipping out of Lucy's grasp and cracking his head on the edge of the clipboard hanging on the end of the bed.

'Oh, I don't believe it!' Lucy wailed, lifting him up and hugging him while Nick looked at the little gash on the screaming toddler's temple.

'He'll live, but it needs gluing,' Nick said, pressing a clean tissue to the cut and holding it there.

'Oh, well, at least it's into the hairline,' she said with a sigh. 'Come on, Annabel, we're going to have to take him to see Daddy. Joshy's got a little cut.'

'Leave her here, she'll be fine with me,' Nick said, and she smiled gratefully and hurried along the corridor and out of the ward, Josh's screams fading as she took him further away.

'Joshy's screaming,' Annabel said matter-of-factly. 'He always screams.'

'He's a little boy. They get in trouble a lot, but he'll be fine,' Nick said with a reassuring smile, and sat down on the floor with his granddaughter and watched the ducklings.

'Oh, Megan, brilliant—are you busy?'

She wasn't, but she didn't want to hang around in A and E any longer than she had to. She'd managed to avoid Josh O'Hara so far, but she could hardly refuse to help Ben Carter. She stepped into the cubicle and smiled at the woman. Lucy. She'd seen her on Paeds, visiting Jem, and knew she was Ben's wife. 'Well—no, not really. What's the matter?'

'This is our son,' he said. 'He's managed to cut his head, and we could do with a hand to hold onto him while I glue it, but he's like an eel and the nurses are all busy.'

'I can do eels,' she said, conjuring up a smile, and she took him from Lucy, steeling herself against the warm, sturdy little body writhing against her.

'Shh, shh,' his mother said, holding his hands and kissing them and blowing raspberries on them, and Megan sat down and held the child's head firmly against her shoulder while Ben glued the little laceration.

'Did you make that kid scream loud enough?' a lazy, sexy voice asked as he finished, and Megan felt her blood run hot and cold.

Ben lifted his head and laughed. 'Yes, thank you for your concern. This is my son—Josh, say hello to mini-Josh. We even gave him your name, so don't be too rude about him. I take it you've met Megan Phillips, our paeds registrar?'

Met her? Oh, yes, he'd met her. And seeing her there, comforting the wriggling, unhappy baby, sent a shaft of pain right through him, stealing his breath away.

Megan looked up at him, a desperate pleading in her eyes, but she needn't have bothered. He was in no hurry to have the past dragged out for public consumption.

'We met the other day up on Paeds,' he said, being deliberately noncommittal, and to his relief his pager went off and he was able to walk away.

Away from Megan and the child, but not his mem-ories...

Nick got back to the barn to find Kate there, home after her spa day relaxed, sleepy and looking utterly irresistible.

So he didn't even try. 'Good day?' he asked, snuggling up to her on the sofa, and she turned into his arms and kissed him.

'Lovely. I've been spoiled to bits. Thank you.'

'My pleasure.' He nuzzled her neck. 'You smell nice. Do you smell nice all over?'

'I don't know. You probably ought to check.'

She did, he discovered, although he got blissfully distracted and forgot what he was supposed to be looking for, and it was almost an hour later before he remembered about little Josh's accident.

He told Kate, lying lazily beside her on the big bed with the view of the sea in the distance and wondering when he was going to wake up and find it was all a dream.

'Poor little mite. You ought to ring and find out how he is.' She trailed her hand over his chest and propped herself up, looking down at him with a slightly bemused smile.

'What?'

'I find it really hard to believe I'm sleeping with a grandfather,' she teased, and he closed his eyes and groaned as she slid her hand down his ribs and kept going.

'I was a very early starter,' he reminded her, and caught her hand. 'Stop. I have to phone Lucy.'

'Mmm. You do. And then we need to go to the hospital. I haven't seen Jem all day, and I miss him.'

She handed him his mobile, and he rang Lucy.

'So how's the little hooligan?' he asked, and she chuckled.

'OK. He's running around as if nothing's happened. There's something funny going on with Josh O'Hara and Megan Phillips, though,' she told him. 'Ben doesn't remember him ever talking about a Megan, but she was helping with holding him and Josh came in and Ben introduced them, and there was a definite atmosphere. He said he'd met her on Paeds, but I'm sure there was more to it. Something in his eyes.'

'Don't go there, Lucy,' he warned. 'Lots of

people have a past. Sometimes it's best left where it belongs. Just remember Pandora's box.'

'Oh, don't worry, I'm not going to say anything, but at least Ben's alerted so he can keep an ear open in case of trouble. You never know when Josh might need a friend.'

'You're a good girl,' he told her with quiet pride. 'You've got your mother's kindness. Give the kids a hug from me, and we'll see you tomorrow.'

Kate met his eyes. 'What was that about?' she asked as he put the phone down.

'Nothing, really. They think Josh and Megan might have a past, and not a happy one, judging by the sound of it.'

She frowned. 'Do you know, I was thinking the other day she looked sad and a little lost. Poor girl. Poor both of them, whatever it is.'

She glanced at her watch. 'Come on, Grandad. We need to get a move on.'

'You realise if you marry me they'll be calling you Grannie,' he said slyly, and her eyes widened.

'Well, that's a good reason not to,' she said, but he just laughed and got out of bed, hauling her up into his arms and kissing her soundly.

'Coming in the shower with me?' he asked, and she chuckled.

'Now, there's an offer I can't refuse,' she said.

They took Bruno in to see Jem the next day, after arranging access to the courtyard off the ward with the help and permission of the ward sister and Sid Evans, the ancient and very co-operative handyman, who was only too happy to let them into the garden through the locked outer gate.

Jem was delighted to see him, and Bruno, far from being over-excitable and boisterous, sniffed him cautiously, licked his hand and, when he leant forwards and brought it in range, his face, and then sat beside him, his head on his knee, gazing adoringly at him and moving not a muscle.

'Do you think Bruno realises he's not well?' Kate murmured to Nick.

'I have no idea, but if you told me that, I'd believe it. He's much livelier with me than he is with you, so maybe he knows I'm stronger. He knows I can take it, so he jumps all over me.'

'Yes, and you shouldn't let him! And am I imagining it or did I see dog hair on the sofa yesterday?'

He looked guilty, and she laughed and told him off.

'He's not allowed on the furniture! Especially when it's not ours!'

'He just wanted a cuddle,' Nick said, revealing more of the sentimental side of him she'd hardly known existed.

But there was lots about him she hadn't known. She'd expected him to be a skilful lover, for instance, but he was far more than that, he was patient, humorous and teasing and then, when the chips were down, shockingly passionate. She discovered highs she hadn't known existed, and she just hoped she'd never have to discover the lows to balance them.

Or maybe they'd already had their lows. Maybe now it was time for their highs, their time served, and this was their time.

She hoped so, because to walk away from this was going to be far harder than walking away from him before, and she'd thought that would break her.

But Jem wasn't home yet, and that was the acid test, whether he'd accept Nick being part of their lives, whether he'd accept his authority, learn to take his say-so without question instead of debating every issue to death. And Nick might have to learn to compromise, not something that was second nature to him.

Jem came 'home' three days later, to the barn, and Bruno was overjoyed.

He followed him everywhere, sat beside him, and had to be dragged off to go for walks. Long, energetic walks along the cliffs that helped Nick work off some of the unforeseen frustration. Because since Jem had been home, there had been no long, lazy love-making, no romantic dinners, no casual touches, random kisses in the kitchen, unscheduled hugs that had gone on to become something much, much more.

And he was climbing the walls.

Not that he was any stranger to sexual frustration, but having her so close, wanting her so much, needing her for so very, very long and finally having her there—it was eating him alive.

So he walked the dog, and he went to work to try and forget about her, and every time he came home she'd look up and smile, and the need would slam through him and he'd be back to square one.

But Jem was flourishing, growing stronger every

day, and with the help of Lauren, the physio, he was doing strengthening exercises that helped to keep his body balanced. Kate was still not working, but she was driving Jem here, there and everywhere, loving her new car, and she brought him down to the surgery to see Lauren three times a week, and sometimes, if they were lucky, they could catch a few minutes alone together.

But even though that time alone was short, Nick had no complaints. The crooked little slab pot Jem had made her on the day of his accident always sat in pride of place in the middle of the dining table, and today she was arranging yellow tulips in it, a troubled look on her face, and he left the cooking and went and hugged her.

'He's all right,' he murmured, knowing the pot served as a reminder of how close she'd come to losing him.

'I know.' And she turned in his arms and kissed him, then rested her head against his shoulder for a moment before easing away. Just in case Jem came in. Just in case he saw them and it upset him.

They were very wary about that. Jem had forgiven his mother, her reasons for not telling him the truth had been understandable, but Nick's initial reluctance to accept Jem as his son had left deep scars, and although he called him Dad and seemed to love him, there was still a certain wariness.

But Nick couldn't wait any more—couldn't go on like this, living in the barn and playing happy families and hiding his head in the sand. Jem was now strong enough to go up steps, and soon would be able to climb the stairs. Which meant if necessary they could go home to their house, and he could go home to his, and life could carry on as it had been, with a few adjustments.

It would be down to Jem to make that decision, and it was time to ask him to make it.

So when he got home from work that afternoon, he went and found him. It wasn't hard. He just patted the dog when he came to greet him, and then followed him when he ran off again.

They were in the garden, sitting in the courtyard under a tree, Kate reading a book, Jem doing a maths puzzle—in a book, this time, the games console having been returned to Lucy—and he looked up and grinned. 'Hi, Dad,' he said, and carried on.

'Oh, you're back early! I'll go and put the kettle on,' Kate said with a welcoming smile, getting to her feet and squeezing his hand in passing. 'In fact, I need to ring Chloe. Want to keep Jem company?'

'Sure.' It was, after all, why he was there, and this just made it easier. He smiled reassuringly, and she smiled back and went in, and he sat down beside his son and turned towards him, his arm along the back of the bench.

'Jeremiah, can we talk?'

He put the puzzle book down and looked at Nick warily. 'Why do I always get the feeling that when you call me Jeremiah I'm in trouble?' he asked, and Nick chuckled.

'You're not in trouble, son. Far from it. I want to ask you something—well, several things, really. First of all, and probably most important, are you happy?'

'What, here?'

'Here, with me here, with us as a family—all of it, really.'

'Oh. Well—yeah. The house is great, but I know it's only for now, but us—yeah, it's good. You're a bit stuffy sometimes, and you tell me what to do, but I guess that's just being a dad, and I want a dad, so it's cool.'

Hurdle one, he thought with a sigh of relief.

'What about your mother? Do you think she's happy?'

'Oh, yeah. She's much smilier. She's like she used to be, before she was ill, but more than that, too. Like she's really happy, all the time.'

'And do you think that's anything to do with me?' he asked tentatively, and Jem nodded.

'I guess. She watches you sometimes, and gets a soppy look on her face, a bit like when she looks at Bruno, but sort of more. And I think she likes it that we're all together.'

Nick felt a huge weight lift off his chest, but a sudden attack of nerves took him by surprise and he rubbed his hand over his leg, surreptitiously wiping his palm, flexing the fingers of the other hand.

'Um—there's something else, too. It's sort of a tradition that when a man wants to marry a woman, he asks her father for permission, so he has his blessing first. And your mum hasn't got a father, and her mother lives a long way away, and I was thinking, you're the man in her life, really. So I was wondering, if I wanted to ask your mother to marry me, would you be happy with that?'

Jem stared at him. 'You want to marry Mum?'

He nodded, and Jem frowned thoughtfully. 'So we'll live together always? Like a proper family?'

He nodded. 'If that's what you want, and what your mum wants. But it won't make any difference to you and me, really, because I love you, and you'll always be very precious to me. And I want to be a part of your life, whatever happens, so don't think that if I don't marry your mother, you won't see me whenever you want to, because you will. But we don't want to make you unhappy. We've done enough of that, for one reason or another, and we want to do the right thing now, which for me means spending as much time with you as you feel you'd like, and being with your mother if I can, because I love her, and I always have. I just couldn't be with her before. But if you have a problem with that, then we can talk about it, maybe find another way that I can spend time with her. It's up to you, really.'

'Wow. So if I say yes, we can all be together? For ever? Like a real family?'

He opened his mouth to say yes, but couldn't

speak, so he just nodded, and Jem grinned even wider.

'Excellent! Wow, that would be epic! But no yucky stuff when I'm around,' he added firmly, and Nick had to stifle a smile.

Actually, no, he didn't. He grinned back, and said, 'Absolutely no yucky stuff at all. No PDAs whatsoever.'

Jem frowned in confusion. 'They're funny diary things, aren't they? Like phones and stuff all in one?'

'That's personal digital assistants. This PDA means public displays of affection.'

'Oh. Right. That's OK, then. No PDAs.'

'Except at the wedding. I'll be expected to kiss her at the wedding.'

His son's eyes widened. 'Wow—are you going to have a real wedding?'

'I don't know. I haven't asked her yet—not properly.'

'Are you going to go down on one knee? 'Cos she might like that. It was on a film, and she went all pink and blew her nose.'

'I haven't got that far,' he said laughing, 'but I'll bear it in mind.'

'And she'll want a ring.'

'And a house. Yours isn't big enough, mine's—well, it's in a very busy place, and there isn't much garden for the dog. But—how would you feel about living here? If we could buy it?'

His eyes grew even wider. 'Here? For ever?'

He nodded, and to his surprise Jem's eyes filled. 'Mum would love that,' he said unsteadily. 'And so would the dog.'

'And you?'

'And me,' he said, and Nick forgot everything about PDAs and yucky stuff, and, putting his arms round his son, he hugged him firmly to his chest.

'That's settled, then,' he said, releasing him, and cleared his throat. 'I'd better ask her.'

'I'll go and tell her you want to talk to her,' Jem said, getting up and limping hurriedly towards the house.

'Hey, Jem, I wasn't going to do it now—'

He turned. 'What? You want to wait? Why?'

Why, indeed. He smiled. 'OK. Tell her I'd like to speak to her. I'll be down the garden.'

He walked slowly down across the lawn to the fence, and leant on the top rail staring out over the sea in the distance, twisting a blade of grass into a little circle around his finger and plaiting the ends in.

'Nick? What's going on? Jem said you want me.'

He turned and smiled, and held out his hands, taking hers and drawing her closer. 'Clever boy. I do.'

She blushed slightly and laughed. 'Don't be silly. What did you want?'

'You. In my life. For ever.' He glanced towards the house, and saw Jem standing outlined in the window, the dog at his side. He'd had his orders. With a wry smile, he went down on one knee in front of her, looked up into her slightly shocked, welling eyes and, his son forgotten, he said, 'Kate, I love you. I've always loved you, through everything. You've been the one constant in my life, the rock that's always been there. I need you, but more than that, I need you to need me, to want me, to smile every time you see me, to open your arms to me because you want to hold me, to make me feel whole again. I don't want you unless you want to be with me. This isn't for Jem. He's another thing altogether, and I'll always be part of his life. This is about us, you and me, and how we feel.

'I know I'm not much of a catch—and you probably never thought when you fell in love with me that I'd be a grandfather when I got round to doing this—but will you do me the honour of sharing the rest of your life with me? Will you marry me, Kate?'

'Oh, Nick,' she said, biting her lip and pressing her fingers to her lips as the tears cascaded down her cheeks. 'Oh, my darling, of course I'll marry you! I've waited years for you—I'd given up hope. Oh, Nick, of course I'll marry you,' she said again, so he took her hand and slipped the little twisted circle of grass onto her ring finger.

'This is just for now, because Jem said you should have a ring, but we'll go and get you a proper one,' he said, and as he got to his feet and she fell sobbing into his arms, he turned his head and gave Jem a thumbs-up.

There was a cheer from the house, and she lifted her head and looked up at him. 'What are you doing?'

'He's watching us.'

She turned and looked at him, and held out her arms, and he limped down the path to them, meeting them at the edge of the lawn, and their arms wrapped around each other, the three of them together, laughing and crying and holding on, because finally—finally!—it was all going to be all right...

EPILOGUE

HE GAVE Kate away, their son, so proud, so serious, walking her down the aisle of the crowded church and standing straight and tall beside her, and, when the time came, he placed her hand in his father's with the greatest solemnity and then gave him the biggest grin she'd ever seen.

And Nick grinned back, and winked at him, and then they turned back to Jeff Saunders and made their vows, long overdue but so very heartfelt, and when Jeff said, 'You may kiss the bride,' she saw Nick wink at their son as he bent his head to kiss her, and a great cheer went up from the congregation.

Family, friends, patients—there wasn't a soul there who wasn't cheering this long overdue couple on their way, and Kate felt her eyes fill as Nick touched his lips to hers and sealed their vows with a tender, lingering kiss.

While the choir sang, they signed the register, Jack and Lucy their witnesses, and then turned and walked back down the aisle between all the people who'd come to see them do what should have been done so many years ago.

Her mother was there, mopping her eyes and smiling, and Nick's children, of course—Lucy, Kate's very pregnant matron of honour, with Ben and their children; Jack, his best man, with his growing family and of course Jem, fully recovered and fizzing with excitement and pride at his role in the proceedings.

Nick's niece Charlotte was there with her husband James, and Jess Carmichael, the counsellor who'd helped them all so much, with her 'plus one'. And of course the practice was closed, their on-call covered by an agency because everyone was there with an assortment of babies and children.

Showered with love and good wishes, they walked down between the pews, packed so tightly that Health and Safety would have had a fit, dozens more standing outside or crowded into the doorway, listening over a PA link, and as they came out into the glorious September sunshine, everyone cheered and showered them with rose petals.

Cameras were clicking, everyone was hugging

them, and Kate thought she'd never been kissed by so many people in her life. All sorts of people. Friends, family, colleagues, but others, patients, neighbours, people she'd known all her life, people who'd taken this little broken family to their hearts and made them whole again with their kindness and acceptance.

Nick stopped and looked around. 'Thank you so much for coming. I'm sorry we can't fit everybody for the reception,' he said, 'but if you go up to the Smugglers' and see Tony, there's a drink there for all of you on the house.'

That raised a cheer, and in a blizzard of rose petals Nick and Kate walked down the path, through the lychgate and to the waiting car.

'You're coming with us,' Kate heard Lucy say to Jem, and they entered the car alone, Jem standing with his sister and brothers. The chauffeur handed them glasses of champagne, and as they linked arms and drank and the cameras were popping, the car pulled slowly away.

'All right?' Nick said softly, and Kate smiled back at him.

'Very all right,' she said, and kissed him again.

* * *

'Good party?'

'Fantastic party. It's a good party house.'

He chuckled and slid his arms round her from behind, nuzzling her neck. 'No doubt we'll regret that when he's seventeen,' he said wryly, and she laughed.

'We'll get over it.' She turned in his arms, lifting her face up and kissing him softly in the moonlight. 'I want to be alone with you. It's been utterly fabulous, but I just want them to go now. Is that really selfish of me?'

He laughed quietly. 'No, not at all. I feel just the same. I love them all to bits, but I want them to go now.'

'So how do we get rid of them all?'

'We don't, Jack does. I've bribed him. We're having the kids for them next weekend when they go away. And when the coach turns into a pumpkin, he's kicking them all out. He said we should have gone away, but why would we, when we live here, in this beautiful place? We've waited all our lives for this. I don't want to run away from it.'

'Nor do I, but I wish they would.'

There was a quiet cough, and she looked up to see Jack standing a few feet away, an indulgent smile on his face. 'You need to come for the last dance, and say goodbye,' he told them, and so they went into the marquee on the lawn, swirling round the dance floor one last time before they saw their guests off, closed the front door behind them and turned.

'It's a mess!' Kate wailed, but Nick just scooped her up in his arms and carried her up the stairs.

'It's fine,' he said firmly. 'We're going to Ben and Lucy's for lunch tomorrow with Jack and Alison and all the children, and the catering team's coming back to sort it. You don't have to do a thing. And besides, you're busy.'

'I am?'

'Oh, yes.'

She gave a slow smile.

'I do love it when you're masterful, Dr T.,' she said, and kissed him…

MEDICAL™

Large Print

Titles for the next three months…

July

SHEIKH, CHILDREN'S DOCTOR…HUSBAND	Meredith Webber
SIX-WEEK MARRIAGE MIRACLE	Jessica Matthews
RESCUED BY THE DREAMY DOC	Amy Andrews
NAVY OFFICER TO FAMILY MAN	Emily Forbes
ST PIRAN'S: ITALIAN SURGEON, FORBIDDEN BRIDE	Margaret McDonagh
THE BABY WHO STOLE THE DOCTOR'S HEART	Dianne Drake

August

CEDAR BLUFF'S MOST ELIGIBLE BACHELOR	Laura Iding
DOCTOR: DIAMOND IN THE ROUGH	Lucy Clark
BECOMING DR BELLINI'S BRIDE	Joanna Neil
MIDWIFE, MOTHER…ITALIAN'S WIFE	Fiona McArthur
ST PIRAN'S: DAREDEVIL, DOCTOR…DAD!	Anne Fraser
SINGLE DAD'S TRIPLE TROUBLE	Fiona Lowe

September

SUMMER SEASIDE WEDDING	Abigail Gordon
REUNITED: A MIRACLE MARRIAGE	Judy Campbell
THE MAN WITH THE LOCKED AWAY HEART	Melanie Milburne
SOCIALITE…OR NURSE IN A MILLION?	Molly Evans
ST PIRAN'S: THE BROODING HEART SURGEON	Alison Roberts
PLAYBOY DOCTOR TO DOTING DAD	Sue MacKay